DEATH ON THE HALF SHELL

DONNA WALO CLANCY

Copyright © 2020 Donna Walo Clancy
Death on the Half Shell
By Donna Walo Clancy

All characters and events in this book are a work of fiction. Any similarities to anyone living or dead are purely coincidental. Donna Walo Clancy is identified as the sole author of this book.

All rights reserved. No part of this publication may be reproduced, stored in a retrieval system, or transmitted in any form or by any means, except for brief quotations in printed reviews, without the prior permission of the author.

Cover Design by Melissa Ringuette of Monark Design Services
Rogena Mitchell-Jones, Literary Editor & Interior Design
RMJ Manuscript Service www.rogenamitchell.com

ISBN-13: 979-8664286168 [Paperback]

DWC PUBLISHING

DWC BOOKS
Printed in the U.S.A.

I would like to take this time to thank my bosses, John Vincent Jr. and Beth Francis. They provide me with a job every summer and afford me the time off in the winter to write. It is appreciated more than they will ever know.

1

The March winds were blowing across the point, whipping sand against the glass sliders that Jay stood in front of drinking his beer. The snow hadn't started yet but was on its way according to the weatherman.

Angie and Pickles, his Golden and Papillon, were chasing each other around the kitchen, fighting over a chew toy. Jay laughed as he watched Pickles try to jump up for the pig's ear that the larger dog held in her mouth just out of the smaller dog's reach. They both had found their way to Jay because of owner abandonment. He was glad they did, and now he couldn't picture his life without them.

The house had been quiet since his mother moved out. After Bill Swann was arrested for murder, Jay had to find a new contractor to finish his mother's half-built cottage. Bill's partner, Andy Pratt, took over the business full time and finished Martha's new residence two months later than the original deadline.

She moved into her new place at the end of February and was still in the process of decorating it and making the space her own. The dogs had worn a path in between Jay's cottage and Martha's, visiting her every day that she didn't work.

In January, Jay had decided to close the café Monday through Wednesday. Business had dropped off over fifty percent in the winter season. He had to do something to make sure the money made during the first summer open for business would last through the offseason. This so he could make payroll and continue to pay the other bills. He shifted schedules around so that his full-time staff still had their forty hours a week and kept his part-timers working twenty hours. He was trying to keep his business and personal money separate. The café had to survive on its own merit.

Jay stared out over the water. The wind had whipped up some good size surf, just the kind that Robbie loved to ride. He searched the beach to see if he was out there, braving the elements.

Robbie Hallett, Jay's younger brother, was an avid surfer. Blond, well-built and good looking, he always had girls hanging around whether he was working at the bar or hanging out at the beach. He lived in the smaller cottage behind Jay as part of his pay package.

Robbie had put in seventy plus hours a week during the summer working as the bar manager at the café. He was a player and knew how to rake in the tips while he poured drinks. All summer, he threw his tips in a big pickle jar, saving them, investing in a top-of-the-line wetsuit so that he could surf in the cold water through the winter months. He also bought the new Surf Catch board that he had been eyeing for over a year.

Jay slammed the rest of his beer and headed to the kitchen to grab another when he heard a knock at the front door. The dogs started barking. Robbie walked through the door before Jay could get there to answer it. He was in his wetsuit, ready to hit the beach.

"Dude, have you seen those waves? Hey, girls," he said, patting the two dogs.

"I was just watching them. Truthfully, I was looking around the beach for you," Jay replied. "Are you heading out there now?"

"I'm waiting for Paul, you know, the buddy system and all that. I just wanted to let you know that I did a liquor and beer order this morning. I tried to put it off as long as I could, but we really needed to restock."

"Will this order get us through the St. Patrick's Day party?" Jay asked.

"It should. I think what I ordered will get us through to the end of the month," Robbie answered. "I ran into Roland up at the bar. He was looking out through the telescope, watching the point. I think he likes the café being closed three days a week. He enjoys the quiet."

Roland Knowles, the resident ghost, was the lighthouse keeper at the turn of the twentieth century. He was murdered while protecting the location of the pirate's treasure that he had found and reburied somewhere on the property.

Much of the time, he spent in the lighthouse, watching, protecting ships from dangerous rocks off the point. He did like to occasionally show himself to the customers who were eating in the café when he felt like having some fun at their expense.

"Any news on the emerald jewelry yet?" Robbie asked. "Didn't you have a meeting with your attorney yesterday?"

"Yes, I did. He finally heard from the private investigator that he hired over in Spain to dig into Duchess Sophia's family history. There is no record of any relatives before she married, and her husband was murdered before she even left Spain. She received the emeralds as a wedding gift, so they were her sole property. Her only daughter died in the shipwreck of The Fallen Mist. There are no living relatives that can lay claim to the jewelry, and neither can the Spanish government."

The previous December, when Jay solved a hundred-year-old mystery, he discovered the missing Duchess Sophia's bones and her cache of emerald jewelry that had been buried with her. Sixteen pieces, each one with emeralds of varying sizes and set in gold, were worth a fortune in today's time.

"That's awesome news. That means finders keepers, losers' weepers," Robbie chuckled. "Did you have it appraised yet?"

"Not yet. I didn't want to jump the gun until I knew if it was mine or not. Now that I know, I am going to have an appraiser come to the cottage and have the appraisal done here. I don't want to let the emeralds out of my sight," Jay admitted.

"Don't blame you, dude. We are talking millions here. I wouldn't let them out of my sight either. Are you going to have Boyd stand guard when it's being done?" Robbie asked.

"It will be done in secret, but yes, I probably will have the sheriff and maybe Deputy Nickerson stand guard just to be on the safe side," Jay replied.

"Cool. Let me know when it's happening. I'd like to watch. Paul just drove up the hill. Time to catch some waves. Talk at you later," Robbie said, closing the door behind him.

Jay grabbed another beer and returned to the sliders to watch his brother. Robbie and Paul paddled out and sat on their boards, waiting for the bigger waves to roll in. They both had been surfing for many years and were good at it. Jay had tried surfing several different times but didn't get the same enjoyment out of the sport that his younger brother did. He finished his beer and went upstairs to his office, dogs in tow.

The mail had piled up for several days. When George Peterson found out that his children abandoned his beloved dog, Angie, he wrote them out of his will. He created a trust to help animals and made Jay the only trustee to the money. His children vowed to fight the will and get the money back.

Somehow, word had leaked out that Jay had been put in control of the trust, and now he was receiving at least a dozen letters a week asking for help and donations. He would read the requests over, and if it seemed that the need was there, he would send a check. The other letters he kept in a file for the future.

Separating the remaining mail into café and personal piles, he sat back in his chair, staring at the unopened envelopes. He picked up his mail first and flipped through the stack. One envelope caught his attention. It had no return address, and the writing looked like it had been carefully written to disguise the real handwriting of the sender.

Jay slit open the top of the envelope, and a small amount of white powder spilled out. He dropped the envelope on the desk and jumped out of his chair. Shooing the dogs out of the office and into his bedroom, he closed the door behind them. Pulling out his cell phone, he called Sheriff Boyd and explained the situation. He instructed Jay to stay out of the room and that they would be over immediately.

Next, he called his mother to come and get the dogs. He closed the office door and released the dogs from his bedroom. He picked up

Pickles and ordered Angie to go down the stairs. The dogs were leashed and waiting at the back door when Martha arrived.

"What is going on?" his mother asked.

"I'm not sure. I opened a piece of mail, and a white powder fell out. I need you to take the dogs while the sheriff and his men come to check it out," Jay explained.

"White powder? What do you think it is?" Martha asked, taking the dog's leashes.

"I don't have any idea, but I am not taking any chances," he answered.

"Be careful, son. Call me when you know anything. Come on, girls," she replied, leading the dogs to the door.

Jay stood at the front door, waiting for the sheriff to arrive. He hadn't looked at the postage mark to see where the envelope had originated. Again, he was getting soft and losing his attorney's edge.

He had made many enemies in the short time that he had been a working attorney in Boston. High profile cases tended to lead to furious people on the losing side, issuing threats and promising to get even. This could have come from any one of those people, or it could also mean that the Peterson siblings still hadn't given up on reclaiming their father's estate.

Sheriff Boyd's vehicle pulled up along with another cruiser. A white box truck with big red letters on the side identifying it as a hazmat vehicle pulled up next. The sheriff walked over and talked to the two men who were pulling white suits out of a side compartment. Jay stepped out on the front porch waiting to talk to Boyd.

"I thought we would get through the winter without you getting into some kind of trouble," the sheriff lectured, approaching Jay.

"What can I say?" he replied, shrugging his shoulders.

They waited for the men to finish suiting up and entered the house. Jay told them where the letter was located on the second floor.

"Did you get any of the white substance on you or breath it in?" one of the hazmat men asked.

"I don't believe so," Jay answered. "The small amount that fell out landed on the desk."

They hooked up their headgear and walked upstairs.

"Any ideas who sent it?" Boyd asked.

"None, although my first thought was the Petersons," Jay replied.

"I thought they gave up by now and moved on."

"A million dollars will make people do funny things," Jay said.

"This is not funny," Boyd stated.

Robbie came busting through the front. He stopped just short of crashing into his brother and the sheriff.

"What is going on?" he asked, short of breath. "Jay, are you okay?"

"Did you not see the hazmat truck out there? You might have exposed yourself to something by busting in here as you did," the sheriff warned.

"Sorry, I was only thinking about my brother," Robbie admitted, glancing around. "Did I expose myself to something?"

"We don't know yet," Boyd answered.

"You're making a puddle on my floor," Jay said, trying to break the tension.

"Sorry, dude. I'll grab a towel," Robbie said, heading for the bathroom.

The white-suited men came down the stairs holding clear hazmat bags. The envelope and letter were each in a separate bag. Larger bags contained the desk blotter and other items that were on the desktop close to where the substance spilled.

"We don't think this is a real threat according to the letter, but we need to go test the substance in the lab in the truck. We have taped off the door, and no one can enter the room," he advised. "Stay downstairs for now."

"What does the letter say?" Jay asked.

The bag was held up for Jay and the sheriff to read. In the middle of a plain white paper were cut out magazine letters stating, *Next time it will be real.*

"Thanks," Boyd said. "We'll be waiting to hear back from you."

Robbie opened the door for them as they left the house.

"What did they say?" he asked as he wiped up the water off the floor.

"They don't think the substance is a real threat, but we have to wait to see what they say after they test the white powder," Boyd replied.

"Do you think it was the Petersons?" Robbie asked.

"That was my first thought, too," Jay replied.

"Where are the dogs? Are they okay? They didn't get too close to the substance, did they?" Robbie asked, noticing that they weren't around.

"They're at Mom's," Jay replied. "They're fine. They were both on the other side of the room when I opened the letter."

"I could use a beer. Anyone else?" Robbie said, heading for the kitchen.

"Why are you so calm about all this?" Boyd asked Jay.

"Truthfully, I don't know. When did the town get a hazmat truck?"

"It was obtained through a state grant for the lower Cape to use. I never thought we would have to use it here in Anchor Point," Boyd stated. "Things sure are changing fast in our small area."

Robbie returned from the kitchen and handed his brother a beer. They watched the activity in the back of the truck through the small window. Twenty minutes later, the men exited without their suits on which was a good sign to the three men waiting for an answer.

"It's baby powder. There is no danger," one of the men claimed. "Someone has a sick sense of humor if you ask me."

"We need the envelope and letter to dust for fingerprints," the sheriff requested.

"This is a federal case. Whoever did this used the United States mail to send the threat. Our office will forward any information that we uncover, including fingerprint identification."

"Can you at least tell me where the letter was mailed from?" Jay requested.

"Follow us to the truck."

The clear bag was held up so Jay could see the front of the envelope. The letter had been postmarked in Anchor Point.

"That definitely makes me lean towards the Petersons," Boyd stated, looking over Jay's shoulder at the postmark.

"I can't think of anyone else who would do it," Jay said.

"Sheriff, we're going to head out. You can take down the tape off the office door upstairs. We'll be in touch."

They watched the truck pull away. Boyd happened to glance up at the lighthouse and saw Roland staring down from the catwalk.

"We're being watched," he commented to the other two.

"I'm sure he'll pop in later to find out what was going on," Jay said, looking up.

"I need to head home. I have to shower and get dressed for a hot date tonight," Robbie said, smiling.

"Another one of your bar bunnies?" Jay asked, chuckling.

"No! Her name is Amy, and she's a fellow surfer. She has surfed all over the world and is one cool chick," Robbie beamed. "She and her friend were out on the point surfing the other day when Paul and I were. We got talking on the beach, and now we are double dating tonight."

"Have a great time. I, on the other hand, have to get back to work," the sheriff stated. "Don't say a word to the Petersons, Jay. Let us handle it."

"I won't. Before you go, I am having the emeralds appraised here at the house next Monday. A specialist is coming down from Boston, and I would appreciate it if you and Deputy Nickerson could be here while the meeting takes place. It should take no more than an hour or so. I'd feel better with a little firepower around while the emeralds are out in the open."

"Give me a call Monday morning to remind me. Nickerson should be back from vacation by then," Boyd answered.

"Thanks. I'll talk to you then."

"I'm out of here. I'll see you at the café on Thursday," Robbie said, heading out the back door.

Jay locked up the cottage. Small flakes of snow were just starting to fall as he walked to his mom's place to explain what happened and to bring his furry roommates back home now that it was safe to do so.

Tonight, he would take the journal out of the safe and try to figure out where the treasure was hidden. It was an excellent night to stay in and do some reading in front of a roaring fire.

2

St. Patrick's Day was drawing near. Not many places were open in the dead of winter on Anchor Point. So when it was advertised that the café would be having a party for the holiday, the reservations began to roll in.

Twenty-five dollars per person got you an unlimited food buffet, coupons for two green beers, and entry into the drawings for the hourly raffles. Anyone could come to the bar for a drink to celebrate as the café was still open to the public, but you would have to purchase anything you ate or drank. Eighty-four reservations had already been confirmed.

The buffet would include the traditional Irish dinner of corned beef and cabbage as well as other Irish appetizers. For those who wanted something different, seafood dishes and American appetizers that the café was known for would also be served. At either end of the center tables would be smaller tables that offered a full raw bar and desserts.

Robbie had hired an Irish band from Boston, Pots of Gold, to play at the party. The regular diners would be seated on the first floor while the second floor would be reserved for the party. Robbie, Paul, and Pam would handle the bar while three other employees kept the buffet full. Jay would be a traveler and go where needed while Kathy oversaw the downstairs business. With preparations for the party under control, Jay could concentrate on finishing what was left to do for the opening of the new museum.

Over the last couple of months, many hours were spent on the final preparations for the Tunnel of Ships. Information on the ship pieces and the items that washed ashore had been obtained by talking to Roland. He had been alive and originally collected the items. Extended hours were also spent on the internet researching the ships.

Plaques had been engraved with the information and attached to the tables in front of each section. A sheet of plexiglass had been placed over the plaques to keep them protected. There were a few items placed in a separate section that could not be identified as Roland could not remember what ships the pieces had come from.

The center of the tunnel and the largest section was dedicated to The Fallen Mist. The ship had wrecked off the point at the turn of the century in one of the worst storms the area had seen in over a hundred years. All lives were lost in the wreck, except for the Duchess Sophia of Spain. She had managed to make it to shore alive and wandered around in the stormy night, trying to find her daughter, Lady Colletta.

Roland Knowles had always blamed himself for the wreck as the light went out in the lighthouse, and he could not get it relit in the fierce gale winds. For over one hundred years, he watched Colleen's ghost, the name listed on the ship's manifest for Lady Colletta, wander the point looking for her mother. Finally reunited and crossing over, Roland and the three pirate ghosts were the only remaining spirits on the property, as far as Jay knew.

Track lighting ran the entire length of the tunnel, and small buttons were installed on each table so people could listen to what was printed on the plaques instead of reading them.

A booth had been built just inside the tunnel door for the collection of entry fees. Next to the booth, a small case of unbreakable glass had been constructed to showcase the single pirate coin that Jay had found in the tunnel.

The museum was ready for public viewing. The grand opening would be held on the second Saturday of April and be open for the week of school vacation. It would then close again until Memorial Weekend when it would open full time for the summer. The only thing left to do was to go to the printers to pick up the brochures that would be given out to each visitor as they entered the museum.

The sun was out, and the roads were clear. Jay decided to venture to the Burger Box for lunch and to see if there was any word on Cindy. He hadn't called or tried to get in touch with her like she had requested when she moved to Florida with her parents. This did not stop him from checking up on her through her other family members that still owned and ran the local restaurant.

He let the dogs out before he left for lunch. As he stood at the sliders watching the dogs frolicking outside, Roland glimmered in next to him.

Is everything okay?

"Everything is fine, Roland," Jay replied.

I saw the police... and Martha took the dogs...

"Someone sent me a threatening package in the mail, and we don't know who it was. The dogs are fine, and Sheriff Boyd is looking into the matter."

This world is so different...

"Yes, it is, my friend. People are not as friendly as they were in your time. Then again, you lost your life in the name of money, so it was not exactly easy going back then either. Money does funny things to people. Speaking of money, I was reading through your journal last night, and I have started putting the clues together," Jay told the ghost.

You will never find the treasure...

"Oh, I will find it. I love a good challenge, my friend. I haven't started checking out the watch yet, that's next," Jay replied.

My watch...

"You told me yourself that it holds the key to finding the treasure."

I should never have said that...promised Martha.

"It's too late for that now. The treasure hunting bug has bitten me since I found the emeralds, and I will continue to hunt for your treasure. It's the sport of it now," Jay stated.

I won't make it easy...

"I didn't figure that you would," Jay chuckled as he opened the door and called the dogs.

Roland shimmered out as the dogs came barreling through the door. They sat in front of the kitchen sink, waiting for the treats they always received after going out and attending to business. The dogs were laying on their dog beds happily eating their bones as Jay left the cottage.

The Burger Box was one of the few places open year-round for lunch. The place was packed with town workers and locals who just wanted to get out of the house and break the monotony of being stuck at home in the winter. Jay found an empty stool at the far end of the counter.

"Well, look what the cat dragged in. We haven't seen much of you since Cindy left," Ellie, the waitress commented as she filled Jay's water glass.

"Speaking of Cindy, how is she doing?" Jay asked, picking up the menu that had been laid in front of him.

"Not my place to say, but Craig will be back from Florida in a couple of days, and you can ask him then," Ellie answered. "Do you want a few minutes to look over the menu?"

"Please," Jay replied, returning his gaze to the open menu.

He scanned the menu but wasn't really reading it. Why was everyone so secretive about Cindy? All he wanted to know was how she was doing, and no one would answer his questions. He had honored Cindy's request and not called her or tried to get in touch with her. Even his mother had told him to move on, as that was what Cindy wanted.

"Do you know what you want?" Ellie asked, returning from the kitchen and breaking his train of thought.

"Yes, I will have a bowl of seafood chowder and a house salad with Russian dressing, please," Jay replied.

"And your usual root beer?"

"Please," he replied, handing her the closed menu.

While he waited for his food, Jay people watched. It was one of his favorite things to do since he was a young boy. As an attorney, he had to observe people and their reactions to make split-second judgments as to what question to ask next or to decide to move to another line of questioning. He had got quite good at reading people.

In a far corner booth, the local jeweler, Phil Cook, his wife, Stella, and a lady unfamiliar to Jay were arguing. Jay couldn't hear what was being said, but it appeared that Phil's wife was mighty upset about something. Phil continued to eat his sandwich, occasionally nodding to show his wife that he was listening to her.

"I don't know how that poor man survives day to day," Ellie said, leaning in closer to Jay so that no one else would hear her. "It's no wonder he puts in seventy hours a week at the jewelry store. I think it's the only place he gets any peace and quiet."

"He does appear to be hen-pecked," Jay agreed. "Who is the woman with them? I don't think I have seen her before."

"That is Stella's sister, Mary. She is here visiting from Boston. She came for a vacation at the beginning of the summer and never left. Word has it that she has moved in with them. Mary is worse than Stella when it comes to belittling Phil. She has no use for him what-so-ever."

"Poor guy," Jay mumbled.

"Orders up!" sounded a voice from the kitchen. "Ellie!"

3

The waitress hurried away. Jay glanced over at the corner booth again, and this time his eyes met with Phil's. The jeweler put his sandwich down and walked toward the counter. He sat on the stool next to Jay that had just been vacated.

"How is the winter treating you?" Phil asked.

"Good, and you?" Jay replied.

"Slow, but then again, it always is offseason. I was wondering if you had given anymore thought to showing the emerald collection in my jewelry store," Phil said, looking over at his wife and her sister. "It would mean a huge boost in business for me."

"I don't know yet. I am having it appraised this coming Monday by a gemologist from Boston. I don't know if your store could provide the type of security system that it would need to protect the collection," Jay answered, honestly. "When I originally offered, I had no idea that the collection was worth so much and how many pieces would be found."

"I was hoping that you would let me appraise the emeralds. I have been researching this collection for over thirty years and am very familiar with every piece," Phil stated.

"I'm sorry. This guy was referred to me by a jeweler I knew when I lived in Boston. He has traveled all over the world to appraise exclusive collections and came highly recommended. If you would like to come to the appraisal, I can call you on Monday to give you a time and where it will be," Jay offered.

"I would really like to be there," Phil replied. "Thank you."

"You have to promise not to tell anyone where you are going or why," Jay stated.

"I know it's hard to trust me after the last problem we had, but I won't breathe a word to anyone, I promise," Phil confirmed. "Not even my wife."

"Phillip!" his wife hollered above the noise of the restaurant. "Come finish your lunch. We're not going to wait all day for you."

"I have to go," Phil said, shoulders sagging. "Thank you for your offer. I will be waiting to hear from you."

He slowly walked back to his booth, and the second he sat down, the henpecking started. Jay felt bad for the guy. Being married to a woman like that must wear a man down, and then to have a second woman thrown in the mix must have been almost unbearable for Phil. It made Jay wonder if the marriage had always been like that or if it had just gotten worse over the years.

He thought about his own relationships as he ate his chowder. He loved Cindy, but years ago, he moved to Boston and left her high and dry with no explanation because he was afraid of commitment. Now, when he ready to commit, she moved to Florida to take care of her failing parents. She told him to move on, but he was having a hard time with that request.

Then there was Susan. They had dated many times and had much in common. She loved to cook and did a great job managing the kitchen at the café. She and his mother got along great, and it was Martha who suggested to Jay that they get together. Susan was adventurous, had a great sense of humor, and was beautiful to look at. So why couldn't Jay get over Cindy and move on with Susan?

"Here's your salad," Ellie said, placing it in front of him. "You looked like you were a million miles away just then. Everything okay?"

"Yeah, just doing some heavy thinking," Jay replied.

"We all have to do that once in a while," Ellie agreed, walking away to leave Jay to eat his lunch and return to his thoughts.

A half an hour later, Jay left the Burger Box and headed back to the beach on the point. It was cold, but he needed to spend that time walking and listening to the waves lapping onto the shore caused by the winter winds. As he walked, he decided to try one more time to get in touch with Cindy, and if she still didn't respond, he would have to move on.

He returned to the café, ready for a hot cup of coffee. His mom, Robbie, and Craig Nickerson, Cindy's younger brother, were sitting in the waiting area just inside the door.

"They've been waiting for you," Kathy, the head hostess, whispered to Jay.

"What's up? Craig, nice to see you back," Jay said as he walked up to the group. "How was your vacation?"

His questions were met with solemn faces.

"Jay, come sit down," his mother requested.

Jay sat down next to his mother. He knew something was wrong because no one was answering his questions.

"What's going on?" Jay asked, suspiciously.

"Son, we have some bad news. Craig has some bad news, and you need to listen," his mom said, putting her hand on his.

"Cindy! Something has happened to Cindy, hasn't it?" Jay asked.

"Let me start at the beginning, Jay. When Cindy moved to Florida, it wasn't because of our parents. Yes, Dad did die unexpectedly while she was down there, but that was not her true purpose for leaving. Cindy was sick, very sick. I won't go into detail, but she knew she wasn't going to live for very much longer, and she didn't want the people around her to watch her waste away. She didn't want everyone's pity, so she kept the whole ordeal to herself," Craig said sadly.

"Is she...?" Jay stammered.

"I went down this week because the doctor called me and told me to get there as soon as I could. Cindy passed away two days ago, Jay."

Jay's eyes filled with tears.

"Why didn't she tell me? I would have taken time off and stayed with her," Jay said.

"That was exactly what she knew you would do, and she didn't want that," Craig replied. "She wanted to be remembered for her bubbly self and not what she looked and acted like at the end. You have to respect her for that."

"I'm so sorry, Jay," his mom said quietly.

"She could have told me…"

"Cindy wanted to be buried in the family plot down in Florida next to Dad. She didn't want any memorial service or anything up here. All she wanted was a notice in the paper, and she wrote what she wanted to be published," Craig added. "It will run in tomorrow's paper. Jay, I wanted to tell you first, personally, before you saw it in the paper or heard the talk around town."

"I appreciate that, Craig. If you'll all excuse me," Jay stated, standing up.

"Are you going to be okay?" Martha asked.

"I guess. I'll talk to you later, Mom," Jay said, disappearing out the front door.

The truth was, Jay didn't want to cry in front of everyone gathered there. This news hit him out of the blue, and he was in no way ready to hear about Cindy being sick or that she had died. He ran up the beach, the sand and wind stinging his face, and collapsed behind a dune.

He doesn't remember how long he sat there and cried or how cold he had become in the winter winds. He was already numb because of the news he had just received from Craig. Jay wished he had followed his gut and gone down to see her even if she didn't want him to. Now he understood everything. She told Jay to move on with his life because she knew she wouldn't be there to be a part of it.

He opened his swollen eyes to see Susan standing in front of him.

"Are you okay? Your mom wanted me to check on you," she yelled through the howling wind. "You've been gone quite a while."

"Sit with me, okay?" he requested.

Susan sat down, and Jay laid his head in her lap. He was done crying but needed someone just to be there. She sat with him; her arm draped over his shoulder, not saying a word. When Susan shivered from the cold, Jay knew it time to go back. They walked to the café in silence, side by side.

Susan returned to the kitchen to finish her orders for the following weekend's business, and Jay went upstairs to the bar and poured himself a drink. Roland shimmered in next to him.

I am so sorry, my friend...

"Thank you," Jay replied, taking another swig of his drink.

I know Cindy is gone, but Susan is still here and always has been... don't lose her, too.

"I know what you are saying, Roland."

No, I don't think you do. Susan loves you...

"I can't think about that right now. No offense, Roland, but I'd just like to be by myself right now," Jay requested, pouring himself another drink.

I understand...

The ghost disappeared. Jay took the bottle and glass over to the table near the panoramic window where he and Cindy had eaten the night the café opened. He stared out the window, getting lost in the waves that were crashing onto the shore.

4

The days passed, and Jay was learning to accept the fact that Cindy was gone. Susan had kept her distance, giving Jay time to grieve. His mother had confessed that she knew Cindy was sick but had been sworn to secrecy. At first, Jay was mad that she hadn't told him what was going on, but he understood her loyalty to Cindy as they had remained close even when he left and lived in Boston.

Business went on as usual, and the Saint Patrick's Day celebration was only two days away. The café had been decorated in greens and golds with little leprechauns peeking out from every corner and crevice. The parquet dance floor was assembled in the center of the room. The buffet tables were set up near the elevator to the kitchen.

Robbie had fully stocked the bar as this was a holiday of drinking. A half keg of green beer had been added to the line to be served on draft. The food had been delivered, and what could be prepared in advance was ready to go. A table was set up at the rear of the room with prizes to be raffled off each hour. Many of the town's businesses had donated a gift for the table.

With two days to go, there had been one hundred and forty-five reservations called in and paid for to date. Not knowing how many other patrons would show up at the door, Susan allotted for enough food to feed one hundred and seventy- five people. The band would be there to set up at seven o'clock and would play until midnight.

Jay made arrangements with the local cab company to be on call to drive anyone home who had partied a bit too much. He would foot the bill as he wanted no accidents or problems stemming from the celebration. He wanted everyone to get home safely.

After checking with the hostess to make sure all was going fine, he ducked into the kitchen, looking for Susan. She was in the office, ordering fresh produce for the following day.

"Are you off work?" Jay asked, leaning in the door.

"Just finished," she replied, shutting down the computer. "Do you need me to do something?"

"No. I was wondering if you wanted to come over to the cottage and have supper with me," he replied.

"Are you sure, Jay?" she questioned, not sure if he was ready to socialize again.

"I'm sure. How's steak and corn on the cob cooked on the grill sound? We can steal some potato salad from the fridge here, but you must promise not to tell the executive chef. She'll have my hide for stealing food and throwing off her inventory," Jay laughed.

"As long as you're doing the cooking. It's blowing up a gale out there, and you have to be a little crazy to be standing outside cooking," she insisted. "I'll stay inside with the dogs, in front of the warm fireplace with a nice glass of wine, thank you."

"Great. I'll get my coat from the office, and we're out of here. We can walk to the house, and I'll drive you back later to get your car."

"Jay, it's nice to have you back," Susan said, her blue eyes twinkling. "Besides, how much trouble can you get into with the executive chef when she's eating the food, too?"

The rest of the staff were smiling as Jay and Susan slipped out the back door. They were glad that things were returning to normal and that the couple seemed to be back together again.

Jay slipped his hand into Susan's. The wind was gusting and almost took the couple off their feet several times. Jay slid his arm around

Susan's waist to steady her as they walked. Susan couldn't have been any happier than she was at that exact moment.

Even the dogs didn't want to go out to do their business. Poor Pickles was being blown sideways every time she tried to steady herself to squat. Susan had been right. Only an idiot would be cooking outside on a night like this. They decided to cook indoors and had a nice quiet dinner in front of a roaring fire with the two dogs sitting at their feet waiting for something to come their way. This would be a new start for them both.

Jay didn't see much of Susan for the next two days as she was busy preparing the food for the party. He was sitting in his office, entering the payroll into the computer when a knock sounded on the door.

"Come in," Jay yelled.

Sheriff Boyd entered the room and sat down in the chair across from the desk. The two dogs strolled over to greet him and got their due scratches behind their ears.

"The FBI sent me the results from the envelope you received in the mail. They must have used gloves as there were no fingerprints anywhere on the inside piece of paper. And they think that a sponge with water was used to seal the envelope as there were no traces of saliva to collect DNA from."

"Someone was very careful not to get caught," Jay stated, shaking his head.

"We also checked with the post office, and no one can recall processing the letter," Boyd said.

"What about the Petersons?" Jay inquired.

"I spoke with both siblings, and they vehemently denied sending it to you. They said they have moved on and couldn't care less about what you do with *their* money. If you ask my opinion, they are still holding a grudge but won't admit it."

"They made it quite clear in the attorney's office that day that they wouldn't give up until they got the money back," Jay stated. "I guess I'll just have to watch my back until we catch whoever sent the letter."

"On a different note, my wife can't wait for the Saint Patrick's party here tomorrow night. She got her Kelly-green dress out of mothballs and is ready to dance the night away. Between you and me, I think she's more excited about the buffet, especially the raw bar," Boyd chuckled. "She loves her shrimp cocktail."

"I think we have almost one hundred and fifty people coming. It ought to be a good time," Jay replied. "Susan has been preparing the food for it for the last two days."

"My wife can keep the raw bar. Me, I'm heading straight for the corned beef and cabbage," Boyd admitted, rubbing his mid-section. "I only get it once a year, and I'm going to make the best of it."

"Don't forget, I have the appraisal on Monday. It is at ten o'clock in the morning, and you are the only other person besides the appraiser and me who knows the time and place. Maybe you and Craig could arrive about fifteen minutes before that?" Jay requested. "I did invite Phil Cook to the appraisal. He has been studying the collection for many years and knows quite a bit about it."

"We'll be here," he said, standing up. "I have to run. I have a meeting with the selectman to go over my department's budget for the coming fiscal year. At least Sid Swann won't be there trying to prevent raises for my men. Between you and me, the town is running a lot smoother without him in charge."

"I have noticed that there are fewer stories in the newspaper about blow-ups at the selectman meetings," Jay replied.

"I'll see you tomorrow night," Boyd said, going out the door.

"Come on, girls. Do you want to go out?" Jay asked, and the dogs' ears perked up immediately.

They ran to the door leading out to the back of the café. This time of year, Jay could let them out without a leash. He grabbed his coat and opened the door. The wind was still blowing, but not as bad as the previous night. The dogs were running around and playing in the three inches of snow that had fallen earlier that morning.

Jay leaned against the lighthouse foundation to shield himself from the wind while he watched the dogs. A lone rock was sticking out and jabbed him in the back. He moved over a foot and glanced at the rock that was jutting out. From where he stood, it almost looked like a long, skinny finger that was pointing downward to the rock below. Jay bent over and used his glove to clear the dirt that had collected on the lower foundation over the years.

To his surprise, there was something etched into the rock. The more he cleared the dirt away, the larger and clearer the figure became. It was an image of a lighthouse that someone had carved into the foundation rock. Then he remembered something mentioned in Roland's journal. A lighthouse will lead the way was one of the clues mentioned in searching for the hidden treasure.

Jay always thought the passage referred to the big lighthouse, but maybe this was what Roland was talking about. Maybe Roland himself carved the image to help him remember where he hid the treasure. He would have to pull the journal out of the safe that night and reread the area containing that specific clue.

He stood up to call the dogs and noticed that Roland was watching him from the catwalk above. Jay waved to the ghost, who had vanished when he realized that he had been spotted watching Jay uncover the image.

Maybe I am on to something.

"Come on, girls, time to go in," Jay hollered over the wind.

The dogs received their treats and settled on their beds while Jay finished his computer work. It took him longer than usual to make the entries as his mind kept returning to the image of the lighthouse that he had uncovered.

Could it be as easy as the treasure being hidden behind the stone with the carving? No, there were too many other clues in the journal. And Roland said that the answer to finding the treasure was hidden in the pocket watch, not in the journal. Roland Knowles was not a dumb person when he was alive. He would not make it that easy to find the treasure using only one clue.

Jay walked to the window and gazed out over his property. His mind went back to a year ago when he bought the land. Jay had purchased it for the sole purpose of opening the café with the thought of maybe converting the big building behind the restaurant into a bed and breakfast. Little did he know how the land would provide such riches as Duchess Sophia's emerald collection and Roland's treasure.

Jay had a lot to be thankful for. His mom had decided to stay put and not move to Florida. He was getting along with his younger brother for the first time in many years, and he had two awesome dogs that kept him entertained and adored their master. The only bump in the road was the loss of Cindy. But Jay had Susan, who he was becoming closer to each day.

He had decided that once he received the appraisal on the emerald collection, he would use it for collateral to get a loan to start work on the bed and breakfast. He would keep it open year-round for the people who wanted to come to the Cape and enjoy the seclusion of the winter quiet.

"Jay," his mother called from behind the closed office door.

"Come on in, Mom," he answered.

"I was wondering how much extra chowder you wanted me to make for the party," Martha asked, peeking her head through the door.

"How about four extra buckets? That should be more than enough to feed one hundred and fifty hungry people. Unless, of course, the sheriff plants himself next to the pot of chowder," Jay laughed.

"Stephen does love my chowder," Martha beamed. "So, I'll make a double batch today and tomorrow, and we should be set."

"Sounds good," Jay agreed.

"Roland came to visit me," Martha stated. "He wanted to know if you were okay. He was worried… if a ghost can be worried."

"I haven't talked to him since the day we found out about Cindy. I wasn't very nice to him when he came to check on me," Jay frowned.

"He didn't mention it, but he did ask me if it was okay with me if he let you search for his treasure and not interfere to keep you from finding it," Martha commented.

"What was your answer to him?"

"I told him there was no stopping you when you set your mind to something," she answered. "I released him from his promise to keep you from finding it. He did say that he would not help you and that you had to find it on your own."

"I wouldn't want it any other way. The real excitement is in the search for it," Jay smiled.

"Well, back to the kitchen for me," Martha said as she headed out the door.

Jay continued to gaze out the window. He had just enough time to get the dogs home before he had to work his shift at the front door seating the patrons. Looking up at the top of the lighthouse, he saw Roland standing steadfastly on the catwalk, keeping a watch over the rough ocean waters caused by the March winds. Over a hundred years later, and he still felt a strong responsibility to those out on the water.

"Come on, girls. It's time to go home."

5

Saint Patrick's Day had finally arrived, and the café staff was busy with the final preparations for the party. The sun was shining with no threat of a storm for the next twenty-four hours. The roads would be free of snow and ice for driving to and from the café later that night.

Robbie was stocking the bar shelves to their fullest capacity. The beer coolers had been filled the previous day for the beer to be at its coldest when served. Three over-sized brandy snifters had been placed along the bar for tips replacing the smaller ones used on regular work nights. The glass racks were filled and had backup trays of clean glasses ready to replace the ones in the racks as they were used.

At eleven o'clock, the café opened with just the downstairs tables available to sit at during lunch. The upstairs would open for the party and to the public at six. Martha was running around, putting up some last-minute decorations on the second floor. Susan and her kitchen staff were setting the buffet tables, readying them for the coming food that would be served that evening.

By three o'clock, everything was ready. Robbie, being Robbie, had bought a leprechaun suit complete with a large green top hat to wear behind the bar. Amy, his new girlfriend, was attending the party and had a special chair roped off for her at the end of the bar section where Robbie would be serving.

Jay took the dogs home at four. He showered and donned a black pinstriped suit with a green tie that lit up and played bits of various Irish songs when the tip was squeezed. The finishing touch was a green glitter top hat with a large four-leaf clover attached to the right side.

"What do you think, girls?" he asked the dogs. "Am I ready to party?"

The dogs cocked their heads, not understanding what was being said to them. They wandered off to the kitchen, looking for their supper. Jay was feeding the dogs when Roland glimmered in.

Lots of people tonight?

"Hello, Roland. Yes, there will be many people at the café tonight. You might want to stay in the lighthouse," Jay suggested. "And, Roland… I'm sorry I so rude to you the other day at the bar."

"It's okay… I understand.

"I found the image of the lighthouse on the foundation of the real lighthouse."

I know…

"Is it the one you referred to in your journal?" Jay asked.

Not telling… you must figure it out for yourself.

"Okay, I just figured I'd give it a shot. I don't remember if I have ever asked you. Did you know the person who murdered you?"

No… never saw the person before that night. Why?

"I was just wondering. The book at the historical society said that your murderer was never caught. Did you see him on the property at any time after you died? When you returned in the afterlife, I mean."

Not a him…

"It was a woman?"

Yes…

"According to all counts of the story, it was a man."

No…

"Jay! Are you ready to go?" Martha yelled from the front door.

"Coming, Mom! Just feeding the dogs," Jay answered.

He turned around, and Roland was gone. He set the two dishes on the floor, told the dogs to be good, and went to join his mom. He double-checked that the door was locked, and they left for the café.

The downstairs dining room had a few patrons eating supper. Reservations had jumped to one hundred and eight two people in the last two hours. Most of the locals were waiting for the all you can eat buffet associated with the party. Jay took his mom's coat and put it in his office so she wouldn't have to search the coatroom later if she wanted to leave earlier than the party's end. Martha disappeared up the stairs to go check out Robbie's leprechaun costume.

Susan came out of the kitchen dressed in green. She was wearing a headband with little pots of gold on springs that bobbed back and forth with every step she took. She walked up to Jay and hooked her arm in his.

"Well, don't you look handsome tonight?" she said, smiling.

"And you look pretty spectacular in green," Jay responded. "I was just looking over the reservations. Are we going to have enough food?"

"Luckily, I raised my numbers to two hundred earlier this morning when I saw the guest count rising. We'll be fine," she answered confidently.

"I knew I hired you for a reason. You are on top of everything," Jay smiled, placing a quick kiss on her cheek.

Martha smiled from the top of the stairs. As much as she had loved Cindy, she loved Susan just as much. Her son and his executive chef belonged together. They had so much in common. Martha and Susan had talked in the kitchen while cooking, and she confided in Martha how she felt about Jay long before he had even noticed her. Jay had always been afraid of commitment, but Martha knew he would come around eventually and see Susan and how good they were together. She had told the young girl to be patient, and it would happen.

"You should see your brother," Martha announced, coming down the stairs.

"I have to go up and check on everything for the party. Maybe I'll give him a little grief while I'm up there," Jay said, snickering.

"Martha, you have to come to see the fruit basket I made out of a watermelon for the buffet," Susan said, leading Martha away to the kitchen before she could lecture Jay on his last comment.

"Hey, green man," Jay yelled as he hit the top of the stairs. "Can you take me to your pot of gold?"

Robbie looked up from what he was doing and smiled.

"I think I look pretty good. Besides, Amy picked out the suit, and I couldn't say no."

"Ahh, henpecked already," Jay teased.

"Give me a break, dude," Robbie groaned.

"Seriously? You look great," Jay stated. "Has Roland seen you in it?"

"No, he hasn't been around. Too much commotion for him. He's probably hiding up in the lighthouse," Robbie replied.

"That's what I advised him to do," Jay said. "It's too bad. He probably would give you more grief than I ever could."

The elevator opened, and Susan and Martha exited with the first cart of food for the buffet. Silver chafing dishes were lined up and ready to be filled with hot food. The Sterno fuel burned a bright blue underneath to keep the food warm throughout the night.

Two of the other kitchen staff were setting up the raw bar. Peeled, cooked jumbo shrimps, oysters on the half shell, cherry stones, and various dipping sauces were included and sitting in containers of ice. A bucket of lemon slices was added. Trays of different types of sushi would be brought from the kitchen walk-in right before the party started.

Paul, the first chef, was also a pastry chef and had baked a variety of delicious-looking pastries for the dessert table. Jay walked to the table and helped himself to a miniature éclair.

I have to give Paul a raise, and we need to enlarge our daily dessert menu.

Jay returned to the front door area, confident that his staff had everything ready to go. People were already gathering in the lobby area waiting for the upstairs to open and the party to start. Jay walked around, greeting the locals and taking drink orders to help Kathy, who was working by herself at the front door. At six o'clock, the rope was removed from the bottom of the stairs, and the party had begun.

Everyone who had made a reservation showed up along with a few who hadn't. The party was in full swing. Susan and her staff kept the food tables full, and the band kept the people on the dance floor active. Jay kept busy making sure his patrons were having a good time and called out a raffle number every hour on the hour for a prize.

The upstairs was a sea of green as everyone had raided their closets for whatever they could find to be Irish for the night. Green beads had been handed out at the door downstairs to those attending the party.

"This is a great party!" Phil said to Jay, balancing a full plate filled with delicacies from the raw bar.

"Are you here alone?" Jay inquired, not seeing Phil's wife or her sister.

"No, I couldn't be that lucky. They are here somewhere. Between you and me, the farther away, the better." He chuckled, piling cocktail sauce onto an oyster and tilting the shell to let it slide down his throat.

"Well, enjoy yourself," Jay replied.

A little before nine o'clock, Amy, Robbie's girlfriend, approached Jay as he was ready to call out another raffle number.

"Jay, I'm worried. Robbie left to get some bar stock over twenty minutes ago and hasn't returned. Could you please go check on him? He was going to the cellar to get some Rose and Zinfandel wine," Amy requested.

"I'll go find him just as soon as I call the raffle," Jay replied.

Jay passed Susan at the buffet table.

"Have you seen Robbie?"

"Not for a couple of hours. I've been busy in the kitchen," Susan answered.

"Thanks. I'm going to check the cellar. Amy said that he went to get some wine," Jay stated.

Walking through the back area of the kitchen, near the loading dock door, Jay spotted the hat that Robbie had been wearing sitting on the floor. He opened the rear entrance door to the kitchen and looked around outside for his brother. He wasn't there. Next, Jay opened the cellar door and called out Robbie's name. No answer.

He descended the stairs hoping that Robbie hadn't fallen or had an accident that prevented him from returning to the bar. He was nowhere to be found. This was not like his brother to just disappear when he was supposed to be working.

Jay hurried back to the party, hoping that Robbie had returned. What greeted him was the worst nightmare that any restaurant owner could witness. People were sitting on the floor, holding their stomachs and moaning. Others were floating around the dance floor, dancing when there was no music playing. Phil Cook was lying in front of the bar with people doing CPR on him. Others seemed fine and were watching wide-eyed at the ones who weren't.

Sheriff Boyd was directing people to go to a table and sit down. He ordered people not to eat anything until they knew what was happening. The lead singer of the band brought his microphone to the sheriff so people could hear him easier. In the ensuing chaos, Jay forgot all about Robbie disappearing.

Jay and Martha ran to the sheriff to ask how they could help. He asked them to go to those inflicted and find out what they had eaten. There had to have eaten something in common that was causing the sickness, and they needed to find what it was.

"Please! Everyone remain calm. We have ambulances on the way," the sheriff announced. "Where is my wife? I can't find my wife."

"Phil! No, not my Phil," his wife screamed, throwing herself across her husband's chest.

Sheriff Boyd hurried over to Stella and pulled her away from her husband's body. He checked for a pulse, and there was none. He sent the bartender to get some tablecloths that they could drape over the body. Martha led Stella and her sister to a table at the opposite end of the room while the body was being covered.

Jay glanced around the room and behind the bar. There was still no sign of his brother. People that had been dancing around were now falling on the dance floor. Jay rushed from one to another and was greeted with blank stares as he tried to question them.

The paramedics arrived and started to access who needed to be transported first and foremost. The ones with increased heart rate and increased blood pressure were transported first. The partiers with nausea, chills, and sweating were taken in the second wave. All others left when the surrounding towns sent their ambulances as a backup.

Jay didn't have a final count but assumed over thirty people had left sick. When questioned, many had said the only place they ate food from was the raw bar. But many had eaten food from there who didn't get sick, Jay concluded.

Sheriff Boyd was hanging yellow police tape around the perimeter of the raw bar. Jay realized that he hadn't told the sheriff that Robbie was missing and had been since before the chaos broke out.

People were already blaming the seafood for the sickness. One woman who Jay did not recognize was claiming she would file a lawsuit against Jay and the café. She wasn't one of the sick ones but was going to file a suit anyway for stress caused by the event. She stormed down the stairs yelling that Jay would be hearing from her lawyer.

Boyd walked up to Jay's side shaking his head.

"People will file a lawsuit over anything these days. Don't worry, Jay, we will find out what happened here. I'm heading to the hospital to question people on what they specifically ate. Don't let anyone near the food tables," he ordered.

"I won't. I'm sending everyone home with a refund if they request it. I closed the dining room downstairs also." Jay replied. "This party is officially over."

"Good, well not good. You know what I mean. I'll get back to you as soon as I know anything."

"Stephen, we have another problem," Jay stated. "Robbie is missing. I found his hat near the back-loading dock. His girlfriend told me that he went to get some wine from the cellar and hasn't been seen since. Robbie wouldn't just walk away from his job. I'm worried."

"How long ago did he disappear?"

"Right before this whole mess started," Jay replied.

"While I go to the hospital, take a few of your staff and search the grounds for your brother. I'll be back as quick as I can, but I am going to leave a few of my men here to keep order. Too many people left before I had a chance to question everyone who was in attendance," Boyd stated. "You did keep a list of everyone who made a reservation, didn't you?"

35

"Yes, I have all the names. This is going to set the café back financially... big time," Jay complained. "Right now, though, I am more concerned with Robbie being missing and Phil losing his life. Why do things like this keep happening?"

"Let's see what caused this before we jump to conclusions that it was done on purpose," Boyd advised. "It may have been just a bad batch of seafood."

"I ate a little bit of everything off the raw bar and didn't get sick, not even nauseous," Jay offered.

"I don't know what to tell you. The coroner will be coming for Phil's body to do an autopsy. We'll figure it out," Boyd said, heading for the stairs.

Jay watched as the band packed up the last of their equipment. He knew that Robbie had put a check in the register to pay them at the end of the night and went to get it. Susan met him at the bar.

"Jay, I know the food that I served was fine. The raw bar was iced as it should have been, and I didn't do anything wrong that I can think of," Susan said with tears in her eyes. "Is it my fault that that man is dead?"

Jay put his arm around her shoulders and pulled her close.

"It wasn't your fault. You are a great chef, and everyone knows that. You did nothing wrong. I need your help. The party is over, and the buffet tables can't be touched. The food has to stay where it is along with any food in the kitchen that was prepared for the party," he said.

"I need you and some of the kitchen staff to search the building for Robbie. He's missing, and no one knows where he is. He went to the cellar to get some wine and never came back. Make sure you check every inch of the cellar really well, please."

"I'll secure the food in the kitchen and then take several of the guys to start a search," Susan stated.

"Thanks," he said, kissing her on the cheek.

The lead singer came to the bar looking for Robbie. Jay apologized for the way the night went and gave him the check.

"You know, man, I have played in a lot of bars and seen a lot of things, and what I saw tonight looked like those people had been drugged. Especially the ones spacing out on the dance floor. I'm no expert, but that's what it looked like to me."

"Thanks, I'll tell the sheriff what you said," Jay replied.

"Give us a call next year. We'll come back," he said, folding the check and walking away.

"If there is a next year..." Jay mumbled.

The second floor was empty except for the two deputies standing guard over the food tables. Jay informed them that he was going to join in the search for his missing brother. Craig Nickerson had been off duty and attending the party and was already coordinating the search for Robbie.

He sent Jay to check his own place and his brother's cottage. Robbie's place was locked up tight. Jay had a key and let himself in yelling out his brother's name as he walked around, checking each room.

Next, Jay ran the short distance to his own place. The alarm was still engaged, and the dogs greeted him at the door, thinking that he was home for the night. Jay called out Robbie's name several times but didn't expect an answer as his brother didn't know the new alarm code, and it wasn't going off. He gave the dogs a treat and returned to the café.

The place was eerily quiet. Most of the staff had been sent home with instructions to return first thing in the morning. The sheriff and his men would then question them. Martha, Susan, and Kathy were sitting at a table in the dining room on the first floor. They each had a glass of wine in front of them.

Jay hugged his mom and sat down next to her.

"There's no sign of Robbie, is there?" she asked her older son.

"No, not yet. We'll find him, don't worry," Jay replied.

"Do you think that the same person who sent the letter to you is responsible for this?"

"Truthfully, I don't know, Mom."

"That nosy newspaper reporter was here looking for a story," Kathy said. "I sent him away."

"Are you talking about Gabe? I heard he got his old job back," Jay replied.

"I thought he was still in jail," Martha commented.

"No, he's out on probation," Jay stated. "I don't want him here on the café property. He knows where some of the secret tunnels are, and I don't trust him not to use them again."

"Mention it to Sheriff Boyd. I'm sure he'll give him a warning about staying away from here," Kathy suggested.

"Did I hear my name being tossed around?" the sheriff asked, walking toward the group.

"Yes, you did," Martha replied, explaining why.

"I'll see to it that Gage stays away," he assured the group. "Any sign of Robbie?"

"None at all," Jay answered.

"I'm beginning to wonder if Robbie saw something he shouldn't have when he was headed toward the cellar. You did say that he disappeared before the mishap upstairs," Boyd asked.

"That what his girlfriend said," Jay replied.

"Is this the same surfer girl he was talking about the night that you received the letter?"

"Yea, it is. Her name is Amy, but I don't know what her last name is. Robbie never told me. Did he tell you, Mom?"

"No."

"I don't even know where she lives," Jay stated.

Roland shimmered in behind the group.

"Did you see anything, Roland? Do you know what happened to Robbie?" Boyd asked the ghost.

I was up in the lighthouse...

"That's okay. It was worth a try," Boyd told the ghost.

I saw a red motor car...

"Where? What kind?" Jay asked.

It was behind the café... don't know

"Did you see any people?"

No... it moved too fast.

"Someone took my son?" Martha questioned.

Don't know...

"Thank you for your help, Roland," the sheriff stated.

"That's really vague," Jay complained.

"Right now, it's all we got to go on," Boyd replied. "Now for the bad news. The café must remain closed tomorrow until we can collect all the food we need to test."

"Did you get any leads talking to the people at the hospital?" Martha inquired.

"The common denominator seems to be the shrimp, oysters, and the cocktail sauce."

"Stephen, is your wife okay?" Martha asked.

"She was pretty sick, but the doctors said that she would be okay. They are keeping her overnight, along with all the others. She ate a lot of shrimp and cocktail sauce."

"I'm so sorry," Jay commented. "Phil was eating oysters and cocktail sauce while I was talking to him."

"That's one more confirmation. I am going to have my guys bag and tag the items off the raw bar and take them to the lab tonight to be tested. I'll let you know if we find out anything. Meanwhile, I am going to put an APB out on Robbie and the red car."

"Do you think we will find him?" Martha whispered, choking up on the words that she was speaking.

"We'll find him, and he will be fine, Martha. You just keep your chin up and think positive," Boyd promised. "I have to return to work upstairs. Jay, will you be here to lock up?"

"I'll be in the office."

"I can't do anything else here. I'm going home in case Robbie calls. Jay, please call me if you hear anything," Martha requested.

"I will, Mom, I promise."

"I'm heading home, too," Kathy announced. "I'll see you tomorrow morning, I guess."

"Do you need any help with anything before I leave?" Susan asked. "The kitchen is shut down, and the food from the party has been put in the back walk-in, separate from everything else."

"Thanks for all your hard work in the last few days. I'll see you at nine in the morning when everyone gathers for the sheriff to question. I'm just not real good company right now," Jay replied.

"It's understandable. I'll see you in the morning."

Jay walked to the back of the kitchen, where he had found his brother's leprechaun hat on the floor. He opened the loading dock door and flipped on the light that lit up the area. The wind had been calm all day, and there were footprints everywhere in the snow that had coated the loading platform that morning. There had been several deliveries during the day, and the employees entered and exited work through the back door, so it would be difficult to isolate any prints.

He checked out the security cameras next. The one facing the door had been whacked and was facing the ground. Again, there were too many footprints under the camera to figure out who could have done hit it. The second camera covering the area where the delivery trucks pulled in had also been hit to make it face the open field behind the café. Neither camera view would help find Robbie. He locked up the back door and headed for his office to check out the security footage knowing that it wouldn't lead to much information to help with the search.

Jay plopped in his chair. He could feel a headache starting and closed his eyes, but all he could see was his brother's face. The party was a bust, and his brother was missing. What else could possibly go wrong?

Where are you, Robbie? Dude, we just started getting along again. You have to be okay.

6

Two days later, there was no sign of Robbie. Amy had called at least three times a day asking about her boyfriend and always received the same answer; no word yet. Jay had lost his enthusiasm for treasure hunting with his brother still missing.

The appraiser was due at the house in half an hour. The dogs had been brought over to Martha's home so they wouldn't add to the commotion. Jay had removed the emeralds from the safe and closed it again so no one would know the location of the safe in the house. Jay's only thoughts were that Robbie and Phil Cook had both wanted to be there for the appraisal, and neither would be in attendance.

Sheriff Boyd and Deputy Nickerson arrived as promised. One stood guard at the back of the house and one on the front porch. Mr. Wheaton got in from Boston right on time. Jay untied the velvet case and rolled it out on the table before him.

The emeralds sparkled in the sunlight coming through the bay window. Mr. Wheaton picked up each piece, examined it under an eyeglass, and scribbled numbers down on a sheet of paper that he had brought with him. He didn't say a word as he did his work. He spent quite a long time on the necklace, examining each stone.

"Mr. Hallett, I have found a maker's mark on the back of the necklace, but it is one that I do not recognize. I will have to do further research on it to find out exactly who made the set," he stated and went back to work.

An hour passed, and the appraiser was still working. Sheriff Boyd knocked on the front door.

"Jay, we have a call. There's been a three-car accident down near the Burger Box. Will you be okay?"

"Yes, I think he's almost done. I'll keep watch out the windows. Thanks for coming," Jay replied.

Jay watched the two cruisers take off, lights and sirens going. He perused the surrounding area around the front of the house. Satisfied that no one was there, he closed and locked the door. Mr. Wheaton had moved on to the smaller pieces in the collection. Jay walked around, checking out each window as he went.

As he passed by the bay window on the back of the house, he saw a man crouched in the seagrass. The man was watching the house. He realized he had been spotted and took off running down to the point behind the lighthouse. Jay couldn't risk chasing him and leaving the emeralds unguarded in the house.

Jay wondered how anyone knew about the appraisal. Only specific people knew when and where it was happening, and he trusted those few people explicitly. He had never seen the male hiding in the grass before. Jay would have to call Boyd at some point to let him know what had happened in case this guy was tied into Robbie's disappearance somehow.

"Mr. Hallett, I have finished my work. This is an exquisite collection, museum-quality I might add. I will take my notes with me and comprise a final report for you breaking down the value of each piece," Mr. Wheaton advised.

"Do you have an estimated total worth?" Jay asked.

"I would say the collection's worth in the range of twenty-seven to thirty-two million, the necklace being the most valuable piece. Once I research who the maker mark belongs to, the price could go up," he answered. "For insurance purposes, I would insure the pieces for at least thirty-five million."

"Mr. Wheaton, you did use the utmost discrepancy in visiting today for your appraisal, didn't you?" Jay asked, looking the man in the eye.

"Yes, sir, I did. Not even my secretary knew where I was going, per your wishes of confidentiality. Is there a problem?"

"Someone was outside watching the house," Jay commented, frowning. "If you didn't say anything, that means I have a leak in the people that I thought I could trust."

"It wasn't me, sir, I swear. In my business, I must be trusted unequivocally by my clients. They place millions and millions of dollars' worth of gems in my care, and I have never disappointed one of them," he insisted. "My reputation is essential to me."

"I believe you, but I had to ask," Jay replied.

"I will have my completed appraisal to you by the end of the week. I will send it by a carrier so only you can sign for the package," Wheaton said.

"Thank you," Jay said, reaching into his pocket for an envelope. "Here is the payment we agreed on."

"If you ever want to show the collection, call me, as I have many ties to major museums and galleries," Wheaton said, taking the envelope. "Have a good day, sir."

Jay saw him to the door and locked it behind him. He rolled up the velvet display bag and returned it to the safety of the wall safe. Now that he knew the actual value of the gem collection and that someone might be casing the residence, he couldn't leave it in just a small house safe. He would have to rent a safety deposit box at the local bank.

His mind returned to his brother's disappearance. Why would someone want to take Robbie? It had to be the emeralds. Could they have forced the information out of him under duress, hoping to steal the collection during the appraisal, maybe? It could be anyone who had seen the jewels in the many newspaper articles printed around the country. But if they were holding his brother for ransom, why hadn't they got in touch with Jay yet? Nothing was making sense.

When questioned the morning after the party, not one staff member saw anything that helped. No one could remember anyone messing with the food. And Robbie disappeared at the rear of the kitchen. Even the security cameras didn't pick up anything after they were damaged. Before they were damaged, however, the system did pick up the red car parked near the loading dock and caught a partial license plate, which Jay turned over to the sheriff.

Martha and the two dogs greeted Jay at the door when he went to pick up the dogs.

"Everything all done," Martha asked.

"The appraiser is gone, and the café is locked up. Not one staff member remembers seeing anything last night that would help us find Robbie or who messed with the food," Jay replied. "I did see someone watching the house during the appraisal, and when he knew he had been spotted, he took off down to the point," Jay replied. "I had never seen the guy before."

"Do you think it was about the emeralds?"

"I don't know, but the timing would say yes," Jay stated.

"Did the sheriff say if there was any news on Robbie?" his mother asked with a touch of hope in her voice.

"No, nothing yet. But they do have the partial plate number they are running," Jay said, hugging her. "We'll find him, Mom, I promise. If it takes every cent I have, we will find him and get him back."

"Every time the phone rings, I run for it, hoping it will be your brother," Martha whispered. "Everyone likes Robbie, who would want to hurt him? He's just a surfer dude."

"I'll check with Boyd later to see if they learned anything about the car and let you know," Jay promised, smiling at his mom's use of the term surfer dude.

The dogs were happy to run free when they left Martha's house. Jay followed at a leisurely pace behind them until Angie stopped dead in her tracks and started growling. Jay searched the area where she was looking. The same unknown male was hiding behind one of the smaller dunes just past the seagrass area watching them. Jay ordered the dogs to stay and took off after the man. He was nowhere in sight when Jay arrived at the top of the dune.

I had better get back to the house in case he was a lookout for someone.

"Come on, girls," Jay yelled, heading for the cottage.

Nothing was amiss when they arrived home. Jay shook his head, not being able to figure out why this guy kept showing up and watching his every move.

It must be the emeralds. They want the emeralds.

It was starting to snow, and Jay wanted to get to the bank before the main storm hit. He opened the safe and took out the velvet case. He hesitated a moment, wondering if he should also bring the journal and the watch with him. They contained valuable information about Roland's hidden treasure and could not be replaced if stolen. Deciding to keep those two items at home where he could work with them, he locked the safe and rehung the picture on the wall.

He slid the case inside a folded newspaper and tucked it under his arm. Grabbing the manila envelope containing Mr. Peterson's will and the trust fund paperwork, he left for the bank. Anyone watching would see the envelope and not pay attention to the newspaper.

Jay obtained a safety deposit box at the Anchor Point National Bank. The emeralds were put in the box, and Jay left with the full confidence that no one saw him deposit anything but the envelope.

The next stop was the historical society. It had just reopened the previous week as it took a while to replace Bea, who had worked there and been murdered there by her own son. Marie Ramos, another long-time resident, volunteered to take over the running of the building. It would only be open three days a week, Mondays, Wednesdays, and Fridays and no weekends.

Jay wanted to see if there were any more articles regarding Roland's murder. The few that he had already found stated that a man had killed him, but Roland's ghost said it was a woman. He had two hours before the placed closed to nose around in the old newspapers.

"Hello, Marie," Jay said as he pulled the door closed behind him. "Man, the wind is really picking up out there."

"Jay, what can I do for you today?" she asked, smiling. "How's your mom?"

"She's upset because Robbie hasn't been found yet," he answered. "She stays home near the phone in case he calls."

"I heard what happened. I'm so sorry," Marie replied.

"We'll find him. I promised my mom."

"I really hope so. I like Robbie even though sometimes he is a little too good for his own britches," Marie commented.

"What do you mean?" Jay asked.

"I've seen your brother give away his last dollar to someone homeless even though it left him with nothing. He stayed in your mom's cellar because most of the time, he had given away whatever he had to help someone else. He always worked hard during the summer so he could help people in the winter who needed it," Marie commented. "There are many individuals around Anchor Point who have had a meal or received a blanket to fight off the cold because of your brother."

"I had no idea," Jay said, amazed at what he was hearing.

"Not many locals know what he does or how generous he is, and he likes it that way. I don't even think Martha knows just how much Robbie helps people," Marie stated. "He's a Godsend to the homeless. Him and his gold coins."

"Gold coins?" Jay asked.

"He has a system to his generosity. He has gold coins, not real ones, of course, that he had specially made up to help him help others. Some have a B on them while others have an M," Marie explained.

"B and M?"

"Yes, one stands for blankets and the other for meals. The Burger Box and the local five and dime accept the coins. Robbie sets up accounts with each business for the winter, and when he hands out the coins to the homeless, they can claim what they need, whether it be a meal or a blanket. If they are too embarrassed to go, Robbie brings what they need to them."

"I had no idea," Jay said, shaking his head in disbelief.

"Not many do," Marie confirmed.

"Marie, I have to go. I'll be back to find what I need at another time," Jay said, heading for the door.

"You find that brother of yours. A lot of people depend on him to get through the winter months. He's a good man and doesn't deserve to be treated like this," Marie called out as Jay went through the door into the falling snow.

He hurried to his mother's house to share what he had learned from Marie. While he drove, the conversation he had had with Robbie when Jay first asked him to work at the café ran through his mind. He had accused his younger brother of living off their mother and not being an adult. He had no idea what Robbie really did with his money and why he had nothing to pay rent for the cellar apartment. Jay felt awful about their fight that day, but he didn't know what kind of person his brother really was, a caring human being.

Martha was shocked when Jay relayed what he had learned about Robbie taking care of Anchor Point's homeless. She felt as bad as Jay did, thinking that her younger son was just an immature surfer without a responsible bone in his body. Now she understood why he stayed in the cellar all winter playing video games. He had no money to do anything else as he gave it all away to others who needed it more than he did.

"Oh, Jay, I feel just awful," Martha admitted.

"Me, too, Mom," Jay agreed, holding her. "When we find him, we won't let on that we know. That way, he can continue being Robbie and doing what he does."

"If we find him," Martha said, tearing up.

"We will find him," Jay said firmly. "We will."

7

The snow was piling up outside. The café was closed for the day, so Jay decided to do something to help find his brother. He called the sheriff to see if there was any progress on his disappearance, and the answer was no. Even the security footage from the café didn't lead to any new avenues. The red car had not been spotted again in the area.

Jay took out the spare keys to Robbie's cottage and tucked them in his shirt. The dogs had been out and fed breakfast and were now snuggled together in front of the warm fireplace. They didn't even lift their heads when Jay put on his coat to leave.

"I see how it is. It's okay, I'll go out in the storm by myself," Jay chuckled as he put on his gloves. "You better make some room for me in front of the fire when I get back."

The wind had blown Robbie's surfboards off the back deck, and they were disappearing under the accumulating inches of white stuff. The new board was his brother's pride and joy, and if he were home, the boards would be inside. Jay picked up each board, wiped off the snow, and brought them inside the cottage.

As he closed the door and the noise of the storm was muffled, he heard someone moving around at the back of the cottage. He picked up the fireplace poker, raised it above his head, and quietly walked up the hallway toward the bedrooms. He peered into the smaller bedroom, and no one was there. A loud bang emanated from Robbie's bedroom.

Jay burst through the door, poker held high, looking for who or what was making the noise. A window in the far corner was open, and the rocking chair sitting in front of it was banging against the wall.

Nerves much?

As Jay reached around the chair to close the window, he saw a figure in the reflection of the glass come up behind him. Before he could react, he felt a stinging blow to the back of his head.

Half an hour later, Jay woke up. Cold and covered in snow that had been coming in through the open window above him, he sat up. He was dizzy, and he had a massive headache. He pulled out his phone and called the sheriff, who promised to be there as quickly as he could in the storm.

Jay staggered to his feet and closed the window. Grabbing a towel from the bathroom, he held it against the back of his head to catch any fresh blood escaping from his wound. He slowly walked around the house, checking each room, but whoever had been there was long gone. Heading to the living room, his legs gave out, and he fell to the floor.

Jay stirred when he heard the rumble of a snowplow outside the house. The sheriff was banging on the front door calling out his name. In as loud a voice as he could, he told Boyd to come in. Seeing the condition his friend was in, the sheriff called for an ambulance. Of course, this was over the objections of Jay, who had now been helped to the couch.

"Did you see who hit you?" Boyd asked.

"I saw a man's face in the reflection of the window, but it was only for a second," he answered. "Then I got whacked."

"Did you know him?"

"I think he was the same guy who's been watching my house from the dunes," Jay replied. "But what would they be looking for in Robbie's place? He wouldn't have the emeralds over here."

"I don't have an answer. This case gets stranger every day. Still no ransom demands?"

"No, nothing."

"Robbie was kidnapped on Saturday and still no call by Monday. I'm beginning to believe this is more about what your brother might have seen rather than what you own," the sheriff commented.

"Do you think he saw whoever drugged the food?" Jay asked.

"We haven't got any of the lab results back yet to say that someone messed with the food. We should know more by later today or tomorrow morning. But that does seem more plausible where no one has called."

"Sheriff, the ambulance is pulling up," Deputy Ford announced.

"Who's the new guy?" Jay whispered to the sheriff.

"Deputy Donald Ford. He's my sister's kid."

"She made you give him a job?" Jay teased.

"No, he graduated top of his class at the police academy. I hired him because he's good at what he does," the sheriff defended himself.

"Stephen, I was only joking," Jay insisted.

"He specialized in forensic countermeasures. He's also a profiler, which may come in handy at some point," the sheriff bragged. "The kid is good."

The paramedics set their cases down and checked out Jay's head.

"You're going to need stitches," one of them stated, wrapping Jay's head with gauze.

"I'll go to the hospital, but I'll drive myself as I won't have any way to get home otherwise," he insisted.

"I have to insist that you don't drive," the medic replied. "You don't have anyone that can pick you up from the emergency room?"

"My mom can't drive in this weather, but my brother…" Jay's voice trailed off.

"I'll get Jay when he needs to come home," the sheriff said, knowing what Jay was going to say and didn't finish. "Let's go, my friend. Out to the ambulance with you."

"I need to tell my mom what's happened. I don't want her panicking if she sees an ambulance pulling away," Jay insisted.

"I'll let Martha know. You get that head stitched up, and I'll be at the hospital shortly. You should be home in no time at all," the sheriff said, helping Jay onto the gurney. "I'll lock up here after I look around."

The sheriff watched the ambulance disappear into the storm. He pulled out his cell and decided to visit Martha in person instead of informing her by phone. He checked the back door to make sure it was securely locked and then all the windows, noticing the melted snow under the bedroom window.

The only other disturbance that the sheriff noticed was two round rings of dustless space on Robbie's bureau. Something had been sitting in those spots and could have taken by the intruder. Nothing else in the house seemed to be disturbed.

Sheriff Boyd locked the front door and drove straight to Martha's to tell her what took place. She didn't take the news very well, considering she was already worried about her younger son's disappearance. Roland shimmered in to find out what happened to Jay. He had been up in the lighthouse standing watch in the storm and hadn't seen anything. He shimmered out, returning to his post. Boyd promised to call Martha with any new news and then left.

The sheriff arrived at the hospital just as they finished stitching up Jay's head. While Jay waited for prescriptions from the doctor, the sheriff sat down next to the bed to talk to him.

"I searched Robbie's cottage for an entrance point but couldn't find any," the sheriff warned.

"They had to have come through the bedroom window. I was closing it when I got hit. Both Robbie and I sleep with a window open year-round. So, they either knew that already or they stumbled upon the open window by accident," Jay announced.

"Or there is another possibility. They have Robbie, and they have his keys," the sheriff suggested.

"I guess I need to call and get the locks changed on all the buildings that Robbie had keys for. I also need to alarm his cottage."

"It would be a good idea. And make sure that you always keep the alarms set. Are the you-know-what still at your house?"

"No. I got nervous and moved them," Jay answered, lowering his voice. "They are in a safety deposit box at the bank under a different name."

"Smart. Do you know what was sitting on Robbie's bureau? There are two rings in the dust where it looks like something had been removed."

"The only thing I can think of is Robbie's big pickle jar where he kept his tips. I think there was a smaller jar for just coins next to it," Jay replied.

"I think whoever hit you helped themselves to Robbie's money," the sheriff said.

"Robbie's going to be really upset that the money is gone," Jay said, explaining to the sheriff what he had found out about his brother at the historical society.

"All these years, I knew someone was helping out the homeless on the Point, but I had no idea it was your brother," Boyd said, shaking his head. "You just never know, do you?"

"We have to find him, Stephen. A lot of people depend on my brother," Jay stated. "All the years I spent in Boston looking out for myself and my career, he was here taking care of friends that needed it. I fought with him every time I came home about him being a leech and living off our mom, but at that point, I had no idea what he was really doing with his money. I feel like such a jerk right now for ragging on him about it."

"You have to put that behind you. Your head must be in the game right now to help find your brother. I need the smart thinking attorney, not some whining wimp," the sheriff lectured. "Your mother is counting on us to find Robbie."

"You don't mince words, do you, Stephen?" Jay asked.

"No, not when someone's life may depend on it," the sheriff announced.

"Okay, what do you want me to do?"

"I want you to stay close to home in case they call with demands. While you are there, I need you to make a list of everyone your brother knows and anyone who could be holding any kind of grudge against him."

"I've been gone from the Point for a long time. My list would be incomplete. Mom might be a better one to ask to do that," Jay suggested. "Besides, she might feel like she is helping."

"What do you know about Robbie's new girlfriend?" the sheriff asked.

"Not much. I don't even know her last name or where she lives," Jay admitted.

"Has she been around lately?"

"She calls me at least twice a day to see if I have heard anything," Jay replied.

"Next time she calls, get her full name, and where she is living. If she gives you the information freely, she may be calling out of genuine concern. At least then I can check her out,"

"Paul might know what you need to know. He is dating her friend," Jay suggested.

"I'll talk to him."

"Here you go, Jay. One prescription for an antibiotic for the wound on your head and one for a painkiller. Take it easy tonight," the doctor advised, handing him two slips of paper.

"I will. I'm going to sit in front of the fire and not do a thing," he insisted.

"They used dissolvable stitches, so you won't have to return to get them out. If you do get an infection in the wound or your headache persists beyond twenty-four hours, please come back and see me. You are free to go."

"Thanks, Doc," Jay said, hopping down off the bed.

"The storm's dying down a bit. You get in and start the car, and I'll clean off the snow," the sheriff instructed.

Jay watched his friend clean the snow off the windshield. Could he trust him with his plan or not? He felt sure that Boyd would help him if it would get Robbie back from the kidnappers. They had to make a stop before they got to Jay's cottage. The sheriff crawled into the car, brushing the snow off his coat.

"Stephen, before we get going, I have a question and a favor to ask of you," Jay said.

"You promised the Doc that you would go straight home."

"I know, but I was wondering if you would make one stop at Anchor Point Jewelers first," Jay requested.

"The jewelry store? It can't wait?"

"Look, Stephen. No one else knows anything about what I am going to tell you. Well, one other person did, and he is dead," Jay started.

"I assume you are talking about Phil Cook?"

"Yes, back in December, I asked Phil to replicate the emerald necklace for me to use as a display in the Tunnel of Ships Museum. He took pictures of the necklace from all angles and said he would have it ready before the opening in April. I swore him to secrecy, and he kept his word as far as I know. He promised to lock himself in his office when he worked on it during the day and to work at night when no one else was around. He called me last Friday to tell me the job was complete the necklace was sealed in its box," Jay explained. "He was really proud of the work he did."

"Is it at the store?" the sheriff asked.

"Yes, it is. We had an arrangement, Phil, and me. When we started, he had me put an X, a small X, on a piece of brown packaging paper. He told me when he wrapped the finished piece that the mark would be on the bottom of the box in one of the corners. That way, we could both tell if someone had nosed around or opened and rewrapped the package."

"Nosed around like as in his wife?"

"Yes, Phil didn't trust her much. He trusted her sister even less. And now, with Phil gone, I would like to get my package out of there sooner than later. I would really appreciate it if you walked in the door with me to get it," Jay stated.

"You want to instill a little fear in his wife?"

"Not so much fear, I just want her to know that you are around and watching in case she has tried to pull something," Jay insisted.

"I can do that," the sheriff chuckled. "I always felt bad for Phil. Heck, I think the whole town did. He was so henpecked, and it got even worse when his sister-in-law moved in with them."

"I am hoping that no one else knows about the fake necklace. I wanted to use it if they demanded it for Robbie's release," Jay commented.

"I don't know if that's such a good idea, Jay," the sheriff admonished. "What if whoever has your brother knows something about gems?"

"I didn't think about that. I guess that plan is out the window. I would still like to get the necklace away from Stella Cook and her sister before they claim it as part of the inheritance in the store inventory."

"Have you already paid for the fake?"

"I put down a deposit of a thousand dollars. I was to pay the balance when I picked it up. Phil was supposed to give me a detailed bill when the work was done."

"Let's go pick up your property," the sheriff said, putting the cruiser in gear.

The storm had all but subsided when they pulled up in front of Anchor Point Jewelers. A man was shoveling the sidewalk in front of the store. He spotted Jay and the sheriff, dropped the shovel, and ran down the alley adjacent to the shop.

"I don't believe this! Stephen, look at the front window of the jewelry store," Jay exclaimed, jumping out of the car.

8

Sitting in the front window on a velvet display piece was the fake emerald necklace. Jay looked through the window just in time to see the man who had just been shoveling, pointing in their direction. Stella pushed her sister and the unknown man into the office and closed the door. She turned with arms crossed in front of her, staring down Jay and the sheriff waiting for them to enter the shop.

"What do you think you are doing?" Jay demanded as he approached the counter.

"I don't know what you mean," she answered, glaring at Jay.

"That is my property that you have displayed in your front window. Without my permission, I might add," Jay stated.

"My attorney informed me the piece you are referring to is still part of the store inventory until it's completely paid for and removed from the store," Stella replied indifferently. "Besides. I only put it in the window ten minutes ago. Not that I have to answer to you."

"And what would this attorney's name be when I need to send papers for the lawsuit that I will be filing against you and this store?" Jay inquired furiously.

"You have no grounds for a lawsuit," Stella pushed back.

"Oh, but I do. You forget I am an attorney also, and I know the law. I paid a deposit for that piece, and Phil called me to tell me the piece was complete and sealed in a box with my name on it. You had no right to unseal that wrapped box that had my name on it," Jay replied.

"You can't prove that Phil called you," Stella stammered.

"Yes, I can, and I also have the text message that he sent me stating the same thing. You won't have a cent to your name when I am done with you," Jay threatened. "I also have a picture of the marked box."

Stella's sister Mary came out of the office and stood next to her sister.

"What seems to be the problem here?" Mary demanded.

"Jay is here to collect his property," the sheriff said, stepping forward.

"He has an outstanding balance due before I will hand it over," Mary replied.

"Get MY necklace out of the front window, NOW!" Jay demanded, pounding his fist on the top of the display cabinet.

"You won't get anywhere in my store with an attitude like that," Stella claimed.

"Your store? They haven't even completed Phil's autopsy yet, and everything is yours?" Jay asked. "You are a real piece of work."

"Oh, but they have," Mary smiled. "He died of a heart attack, plain and simple."

"We'll see when the toxicology report comes back," Jay countered.

"There was no whatever that report is that you said. Phil's cause of death was signed off as a heart attack, they released the body to me, and he's been cremated. His service is Saturday. We will be spreading his ashes out over the ocean like he requested," Stella replied, smiling smugly. "You are not invited to the service."

"Besides the store and the house, I bet you had a mountain of insurance taken out on Phil, too," Jay accused the smiling woman. "I'll get to the bottom of this, for Phil, body or no body."

"You don't have to take this," Mary stated, putting her arm around her sister's shoulders. "Sheriff, remove this man from my sister's shop."

"I will...as soon as he has what he came for," the sheriff answered.

"Mary, get the invoice for the necklace out of the office," Stella ordered. "I want this done and over with."

"What's this world coming to when the law takes the side of the lawbreaker?" Mary mumbled as she hurried away.

"Who is the man hiding in the office?" Jay demanded while they were waiting for Mary to return.

"None of your business," Stella snapped.

"It is my business when he's been lurking around my property watching my house," Jay stated. "You tell him to stay away from my place."

"Here is the invoice. You have a balance of two thousand one hundred dollars."

"I want to see the invoice before I pay it," Jay demanded.

"Whatever," Stella said, throwing the piece of paper at him.

"Looks to be in order. It hasn't been altered. It's all in Phil's writing," Jay said, showing the invoice to the sheriff. "What do you think?"

"I don't like what you are insinuating," Stella growled.

"Sheriff, can you grab the necklace out of the window, please," Jay requested, holding out a credit card.

"No one touches the necklace until we get paid. And we only take cash now, no credit cards," Mary insisted, looking at her sister for backup.

"That's right. Cash only or the necklace stays where it is," Stella threatened.

"Seriously?" the sheriff asked. "Is this policy for all your customers or just the ones you don't like?"

Stella glared at the sheriff but didn't offer any answer.

"Stephen, will you stay here while I run to the bank. Don't take your eyes off that necklace. I don't trust these two as far as I can throw them, which isn't too far."

Jay returned ten minutes later with the money. He paid the bill, and then he had to ask for a receipt that the women didn't want to provide, even in front of the sheriff. He grabbed the necklace out of the window and asked for a bag.

"Stick it in your pocket," Stella said nastily. "Or somewhere else."

"You'll be hearing from my attorney," Jay announced as he walked to the door.

"Don't let him scare you. He can't prove anything," Jay heard Mary say to Stella as he closed the door.

"Was that really the guy you saw in the dunes spying on your house?" the sheriff asked as Jay climbed into the front seat of the cruiser and closed the door.

"I'm not sure, but I wanted to see how Stella would react, and she didn't disappoint," Jay replied. "I think he was, though."

"I think I am going to do some checking on Stella Cook. It would be interesting to see if she did take out life insurance on Phil and when. Do you happen to know her sister's last name?"

"No, I don't. Sorry."

"That's all right. I'll find out."

"Did you hear Mary tell Stella as we were leaving that it was okay, and I couldn't prove anything anyway? Jay inquired.

"No, I must have already been out the door. Why?"

"I just wonder what she meant by that statement," Jay answered.

"You did threaten her with a lawsuit," the sheriff chuckled, putting the car in gear.

"Yea, I did, didn't I?" Jay smiled. "But why is he watching my house?"

"Maybe they were going to try to swap the fake necklace with the real one," the sheriff suggested.

"No, even they couldn't be that dumb as to put the necklace in the front window for all to see if that was what they were going to do," Jay surmised. "It's got to be something else, but what?"

"I don't know, but I am going to run a check on the whole lot when I get back to the office," the sheriff insisted, pulling up to the front door of Jay's cottage. "Are you going to be okay?"

"I'll be fine and, Stephen, thanks, I really appreciate the ride," Jay said.

"I'll call you if I find out anything. And Jay, stay positive. We will find your brother," Boyd claimed as Jay closed the car door.

He entered the house to the two dogs running in circles around him, glad that he was home.

"Angie! Pickles! Behave yourselves," Martha lectured as she came out of the kitchen.

"Mom, what are you doing here?"

"The doctor said that you shouldn't be by yourself tonight," she answered, taking his coat and hanging it in the front hall closet. "Sit. I made you some supper."

"You called the doctor at the hospital?"

"Of course, I did. I don't care how old you are. I'm your mother."

"Why would I expect anything less from you?" he chuckled. "Wait! Where is my coat?"

"I hung it up on the closet."

Jay hurried to the closet and pulled the fake necklace from the coat pocket. He walked back to the living room with it dangling from his hand.

"What do you think?" Jay asked, handing the necklace to his mother.

"I've always said that it was stunning, but why is it out if the safe?"

"It's fake. It's the replica that Phil Cook created for me to display in the Tunnel of Ships Museum," Jay announced.

"Wow! It looks like the real thing," Martha said, turning it over in her hand and examining it more closely.

"Yes, it does. Phil was quite the craftsman. I had to fight to get it away from his wife and her sister," Jay stated. "Even with Stephen standing right next to me."

"You had to fight to get it?"

"I'll explain it over dinner," he replied, putting his arm around his mom's shoulder.

In the middle of eating, Roland shimmered in, and he looked extremely agitated.

"Roland, what's the matter?" Martha asked.

There is someone in your brother's cottage. They have been there most of the day...

"Do you know who it is?" Jay inquired, standing up and stepping away from the table.

Robbie's girlfriend and some man I don't know...

"Mom, please call the sheriff and tell him to meet me at Robbie's place," Jay instructed, putting on his coat.

"Can't you wait for him here?" Martha asked.

"No, they may get away before he gets here. I want to catch them in the cottage," Jay insisted.

"Be careful," she said, pulling out her phone to place the call.

Jay approached his brother's cottage under the cover of darkness. He peered in the living room window and saw no one. Moving around to the back of the building, he looked through the slider and saw two people seated at the table, eating dinner in the kitchen. One was Amy, Robbie's girlfriend, and the other guy, Jay had never seen before.

"Jay! What do you see?" the sheriff asked, coming up behind him.

"It's Amy and some other guy. What the heck are they doing in Robbie's cottage without him being there?" Jay whispered. "How did you know I was back here?"

"I followed your footprints in the snow. You stay here so they can't run out the back door, and I'll go knock on the front door. Let's see how they react," the sheriff suggested. "I'll let you in through the slider if they don't run."

Sheriff Boyd knocked on the front door, and Amy and her friend didn't make any motion to run. She answered the front door and let the sheriff in who, in turn, let Jay in.

"How did you get in my brother's cottage?" Jay demanded.

"Robbie gave me a key. He said if the shelters were full and I had nowhere to go, I could come here and stay," Amy explained. "I haven't done anything wrong."

"How long ago did he give you the key?" the sheriff asked.

"I don't know. When we first started dating, I guess."

"The fact that my brother is still missing and you show up with a key to his place really makes me wonder if you don't know more about his disappearance than you say you do," Jay stated.

"Just what are you accusing me of?" she shot back, crossing her arms.

"Okay, everyone, calm down. Have you been to the house before tonight?" the sheriff inquired.

"No, I have been staying at the Storm Shelter downtown. They were full tonight because of the cold weather today, so I came here like Robbie said I could."

"And you are?" Jay asked the man standing next to Amy.

"This is my brother, Adam," Amy replied. "He came to Anchor Point to help me."

"Adam Cook," he said, flashing a badge. "I work out of the Feyton P.D. in Connecticut. I'm in missing persons, and my sister asked me to come to help her find Robbie. I just arrived today and haven't got a hotel room yet, so she offered to let me stay here tonight."

"Cook. Any relation to Phil Cook here in town?" the sheriff inquired.

"He's our uncle. My family was all set to come up and attend the funeral services until Aunt Stella said there wouldn't be any. Dad's been pretty upset about the way Uncle Phil's final arrangements have been handled," Adam stated. "My dad could never understand what his brother saw in her. She changed Uncle Phil. He pushed the rest of us away, and he never paid back the money that Dad lent him to start the jewelry store."

"Four months ago, our dad called Uncle Phil. Dad's business collapsed, and he was going to lose his house. Uncle Phil promised to send him money, but none ever showed up," Amy added. "Dad called again, but Mary refused to let him talk to his brother. Truthfully, no one in the family can stand neither of them."

"They are not well-liked around here either," Jay mumbled. "If it's any consolation, I don't think your uncle was a happy man. Maybe he didn't know your dad called. Maybe he wasn't told."

"But your uncle was a good man. We are still looking into his death, even if your aunt cremated the body already. We are waiting on tox screens to come back," the sheriff said. "We appreciate any help we can get to find Robbie."

"Glad to help," Adam replied.

"Jay, can I talk to you in the other room, please?" the sheriff requested.

The two men walked into the living room while Amy and her brother stayed in the kitchen. The sheriff stood where he could keep them in his sight.

"What's up, Stephen?" Jay asked.

"Two things. I think that our friends should continue to stay here until I can check out their stories. At least we will know where they are," he suggested.

"And the second thing?"

If he is telling the truth about working in missing persons, I could use a fresh set of eyes in helping to find your brother."

"Do you think Amy is telling us the truth about Robbie giving her the key?"

"They didn't try to get away when I knocked, and they both seem very calm. I think they are telling us the truth," the sheriff admitted. "Besides, doesn't it sound like the kind of thing your brother would do now that you know his secret side?"

"Yea, I guess so. So, what do I do? Tell them they can continue to stay here until Robbie comes home?" Jay asked.

"I would. If they leave the cottage, I can have someone trail them to see where they go and what they are up to," the sheriff suggested.

"You are going to check out their story, right?" Jay insisted.

"That will be the first thing I do tomorrow morning," the sheriff promised.

"Fine. I don't like it, but I will do as you suggest," Jay relented.

The two men returned to the kitchen, where they found Amy and her brother finishing their supper. Jay had to agree with the sheriff that the pair seemed calm and in no way guilty of anything.

"Amy, I want to apologize. This whole thing with Robbie is driving me crazy. The more I think about it, it might be better if you two stay here and watch the place until my brother returns. Someone broke in earlier today, and if you had been here, it might not have happened," Jay said, trying to sound sincere. "Just don't invite anyone else here, but you two, okay?"

"Someone broke in here today? Did you catch them?" Adam asked.

"No, unfortunately, we didn't," the sheriff admitted.

"Was anything missing?"

"I did notice that Robbie's tip jar and gold coin jar is not where he usually kept it," Amy offered. "They were on his bureau last time I was here."

"Gold coin jar?" the sheriff asked.

"The jar where Robbie kept the special gold coins that he passed out to the homeless that they could turn in for a meal at The Burger Box or a blanket at the five and dime," Amy explained. "Oh, crap, I wasn't supposed to tell anyone about that. He is going to be so mad at me."

"I already knew," Jay stated.

"When was the last time that you were here?" the sheriff asked Amy.

"The night of the party… the night… he disappeared."

"It's okay, sis. We'll find him, I promise," Adam said, wrapping his arm around her shoulders.

Jay watched Amy, trying to use his powers of being able to read people to decide if she really cared for his brother or if the whole thing was just an act. He couldn't tell. She seemed to be genuinely concerned for Robbie, but Jay had seen many acts like this before in a courtroom. He concluded that only time would tell if she was being honest.

"Are you sure you don't mind if we stay here?" Adam asked.

"I'm sure. Do me a favor though, if you see anyone skulking around, let me know," Jay requested, passing Adam a business card with his cell number on it.

"We will, immediately," Amy replied. "And thank you. My brother took his vacation time to come up here to help me find Robbie. I wish I could remember anything from that night that might help, but I can't."

"Are you almost ready to go?" the sheriff asked Jay.

"Yes, just one more thing. Don't get upset if Roland comes to visit you while you are staying here," Jay warned.

"Who's Roland?" Adam asked.

"I'll explain it to you even though I know you won't believe me until you see him for yourself," Amy laughed. "He's really nice… for a ghost, that is."

"A ghost? Seriously?"

"On that note, we are out of here," the sheriff stated.

"Is everything okay?" Martha asked as the two men came in through the back door. "Hello, Stephen."

"It was Amy, Robbie's girlfriend, and her brother," Jay replied. "Apparently, Robbie gave her a key to the place in case she needed somewhere to stay."

"Did you let them stay?" his mother asked.

"Her brother is a cop from Connecticut. She asked him to come up and help find your son. I'm going to check out their stories in the morning, but I convinced Jay to let them stay there to keep another break-in from occurring," the sheriff explained.

"Makes sense. He's going to help find Robbie?"

"That's the idea," Jay replied.

"You sound dubious," Martha commented.

"I don't know. It's just nothing is making sense so far about Robbie's disappearance. No ransom note, no nothing. And it bothers me that I don't know that much about Amy, her friends or her family."

"They did say that Phil Cook was their uncle," Stephen added.

"She seems genuinely nice to me, a bit scatter-brained at times, but nice. If she's someone that Robbie has chosen to be with, then we must respect his choice," Martha insisted. "I made a fresh pot of coffee, and an apple pie just came out of the oven. Who's in?"

"I would love to, but I'm already late getting home, and the missus isn't going to be very happy with me," the sheriff replied. "Maybe next time."

"I'll walk you to the door," Jay offered.

"As soon as I know anything tomorrow, I'll give you a call," the sheriff promised as he left.

Jay and Martha sat in front of the roaring fire eating warm apple pie and vanilla ice cream. Her son ate three helpings to his mother's one. He told her everything they had learned while at Robbie's place. Martha cleaned up the dishes while Jay took the dogs out. He kept them on their leashes as he could hear the coyotes howling a short distance away in the dunes.

He let the dogs back in the house and watched the three pirate ghosts walking along the dunes in their nightly residual stroll. He knew the ghosts had to have something to do with the lost treasure, but what? When they were out of sight, he went back into the house.

His mom was spending the night in his room, so he pulled out the sofa bed. The dogs jumped up on the bed, patiently waiting as Jay stoked the fire, took some medicine for his headache, and then climbed into the bed. Angie snuggled up to Jay's leg, and Pickles snuggled up to Angie.

"Good night, girls," Jay said quietly as he shut off the light.

9

Jay's cell phone rang as he was walking the dogs the next morning. They were enjoying themselves romping in the snow that had fallen the previous day.

"Hello, Stephen," he answered. "You got something good for me?"

Adam Cook checks out. I talked to his supervisor at his precinct, and he did take vacation to come up and help his sister.

"Knowing that makes me feel better. I'm not so wary about letting them stay in the house. Are you going to invite him to the station and share what little information we have gathered so far?"

I wanted to make sure it was okay with you first. The red car was spotted on Main Street this morning. By the time we could get a cruiser there, it was gone. Nickerson rode around looking for it but couldn't find it.

"Well, at least we know it is still in the area. Maybe that means Robbie is too," Jay surmised. "Have you had a chance to check out Stella and her gang yet?"

Not yet, but I have a couple of men working on it. I called the lab, and we should have all the tox reports back sometime today. I'll call you when I know anything.

"I'll be at the café getting some work done. We reopen tomorrow, but after everyone getting sick at the party, I don't know how busy we will be," Jay replied.

If it turns out to be sabotage, I will call the paper and personally issue a statement.

"I appreciate that. We need the business. The Saint Patrick's Day party set the café way back financially. We threw out all the party food and cleaned out the refrigerators of any food that had been stored near it to be on the safe side. This is not the time of year to absorb a huge loss like that," Jay said.

I understand. I'll be in touch.

Jay hung up the phone and glanced upwards. Roland was standing on the catwalk watching him. Jay waved to the ghost, and he disappeared. Deciding to take the dogs with him to the office, he started in the direction of the café.

"Jay! Jay, wait up," Amy yelled from behind him.

"Hello, Amy. Adam," Jay said, reining in the dogs who were jumping all over Amy.

"The sheriff just called and asked Adam to come to the station for a conference. I think he is going to accept my brother's offer of help," Amy said, smiling. "I'm going to spend the day at the different beaches around town and see if any of our surfer friends have heard anything."

"Keep an eye out for the red car. The sheriff said it was seen in town this morning," Jay replied, deciding that he could trust them. "I'll be at the café if you find out anything. The front door will be open."

"Thanks again for letting us stay at Robbie's place," Adam stated.

"Not a problem," Jay answered. "I need to look through all the security videos of that night. Maybe I can spot something I missed the first time I went through them."

"If you want, I can scan through them at some point, you know, fresh eyes and all," Adam offered as Jay walked away.

"Sounds good."

Jay settled in behind his desk. The dogs curled up on their beds, chewing on their new pig's ears. The mail had piled up since the last time Jay had been in the office, and he wasn't too keen on looking through all the bills that were due. He set the pile aside and reached for the two videos that were recorded the night of the party. As he sat back down, he hit the pile of mail, and it scattered all over the floor.

One envelope caught his eye. It was addressed to Jay in red marker. After the episode with the baby powder sent in the previous envelope, he was more cautious this time. He hurried to the kitchen to grab some plastic gloves off the line and returned to the office. He had just picked up the envelope when he heard his mother call his name.

"Stay out of the office, Mom!"

"What's happening in there?" she asked from just outside the door.

"Take the dogs back to the cottage, please," Jay requested, opening the door handing her the leashes. "I received another weird envelope. It may be nothing, but I don't want to take any chances."

"Be very careful and call Stephen and let him know what is going on," Martha requested.

"I will," Jay promised as he closed the door.

He picked up the envelope and turned it over in his hand. The back was clear of writing. There was no postmark or return address.

Well, here goes nothing.

He slowly slit the envelope across the entire top, making sure not to tip it. Keeping it at arm's length, he peered in and breathed a sigh of relief. There was no foreign substance that he could see, just a piece of paper. He carefully pulled the letter out and unfolded it. Jay scanned the red lettering and pulled his phone out to call the sheriff.

"Stephen, you need to get over here right away. I'm in my office at the café and bring Adam if he's still there with you."

Jay set the letter on top of the desk and waited for the sheriff to arrive. He was pacing back and forth when Roland appeared behind the desk.

What's wrong?

"They took Robbie for the necklace, Roland. They took my brother for money," Jay replied, kicking the desk. "I was waiting for a ransom call, and the letter was sitting here the whole time."

"Jay is it okay to open the door?" the sheriff asked.

"Come in, Stephen," Jay answered.

"What the...." Adam mumbled, staring at Roland, who shimmered out when he realized that the sheriff wasn't alone.

The sheriff chuckled.

"Amy wasn't kidding, was she?" Adam asked, still staring at the spot where Roland had been.

"No. Roland is real. Well, as real as a ghost can get, I guess," Jay replied.

"Why the call, Jay?" the sheriff asked.

"We have been waiting for a ransom call, and there isn't going to be one. Look on the desk," Jay instructed.

"You will be instructed where to deliver the emerald necklace. If you ever want to see your brother again, do not involve the police. Another letter will follow," the sheriff read out loud, not touching the paper because of the lack of gloves.

"So, it was a kidnapping for money," Adam stated, looking over the sheriff's shoulder. "Have you checked the rest of the mail?"

"No, I haven't. It's piled up over there," Jay answered.

Adam pulled plastic gloves out of his coat pocket, picked up the mail, and started to sift through the pile.

"Nothing here," he announced.

"Adam, would you go out to the cruiser and grab two evidence bags out of the trunk," the sheriff requested, tossing him the keys.

"Sure, I'll be right back."

"What do you want to do, Jay?" the sheriff asked once Adam left the room.

"I don't have a choice. I'll have to give them the necklace."

"The real one or the fake one?" the sheriff inquired.

"I don't think I can take a chance using the fake one," Jay admitted.

"Don't do or say anything just yet. We need to monitor the mail for another letter, and by then, I will have completed a background check on Stella and her friends," the sheriff stated. "We'll see if we can get any fingerprints or DNA off the letter and envelope."

"Jay! Are you okay?" Susan yelled from the lobby.

"I'm fine. Could you come to the office for a minute?" her boss requested.

"Hi, Sheriff," Susan said, poking her head through the door. "What do you need, Jay?"

"Have you been collecting the mail while Kathy has been on vacation?"

"Yes, I go out to the mailbox every day, about eleven o'clock. Why?"

"Have you seen anyone hanging around out in the parking lot that you didn't know?" the sheriff asked.

"There was one guy on Monday that hid his face from me and hurried down the hill when I got closer to him," Susan replied. "I just figured he was looking for somewhere to eat lunch and left when he realized we were closed."

"Was he near the mailbox?" Jay asked.

"Not when I walked outside."

"What can you remember about him?" the sheriff inquired.

"He was tall and thin and had on an ill-fitting suit coat. I remember thinking at the time it was kind of strange that he had no winter coat on in this weather. His hair was thin on the top and grey in color. Other than that, I have nothing I can add," Susan stated.

"It sounds like my friend from the dunes," Jay announced. "And the guy who was shoveling the walk at the jewelry store."

Adam entered the office carrying the evidence bags. He smiled at Susan, and she smiled back.

"Adam Cook, Susan Myers. Susan is my executive chef," Jay said. "Adam is Amy's brother and has come up from Connecticut to help find Robbie."

"Nice to meet you," Susan said. "Can I go now? I have stuff on the stove."

"Yea, thanks for your help," Jay answered.

"She seems nice," Adam commented, watching Susan as she walked away.

"She is. The mail hasn't arrived yet today. Whoever dropped off this first letter will not come near the place with the cruiser parked outside. Can you take the letter and go so that I can sit at the window and watch the mailbox?" Jay requested.

"Sounds like a plan, but don't go after the guy yourself. Call me if you see him, and hopefully, I can be at the bottom of the hill when he leaves," the sheriff replied. "Adam, I'll give you a ride back to your car. I'll call you when I get the tox results, Jay."

"Thanks," Jay replied, as Adam placed the letter and envelope in separate evidence bags.

"Do you want me to come back and stay with you while you wait for the mail?" Adam asked Jay.

As worried as he was about his brother, he felt a twang of jealousy weld up in his stomach when he thought that Adam was coming back with the intent to spend more time with Susan. But then again, Jay and Susan weren't going steady or anything. They were just dating. If Adam asked her out, there wasn't much Jay could say or do about it.

"If he shows it would be better with two people to confront him," Jay replied, trying to put Susan out of his thoughts.

"I'll be back in twenty minutes," Adam commented.

Jay sat in the front window, peering out from behind the curtain. The cruiser disappeared down the hill, and the mail truck should be arriving within the next half hour.

Who was that?

"That was Adam Cook. He is Robbie's girlfriend's brother and a cop from Connecticut that came here to help find Robbie," Jay answered without taking his eyes off the window. "Do me a favor, Roland. Keep an eye on him if you can. He and his sister are staying in Robbie's cottage."

You do not trust him?

"I'm not sure. I guess I don't know him or his sister well enough to trust either of them," Jay admitted.

I miss Robbie...

"I do, too, my friend. I do, too," Jay mumbled.

I came to tell you that a stranger is hiding in the dunes near the lighthouse. I saw him from the catwalk...

"Is he still there?" Jay asked, jumping up from his seat.

He was when I came to tell...

"Thanks, Roland," Jay yelled, running out the front door.

The two men spotted each other at the same instant. Jay took off in a full-out run to catch the stranger who had disappeared down below the level of the dunes. When Jay hit the beach, the guy was nowhere to be seen. He scanned the water's edge, up and down, and no one else was around.

How did he get away so fast?

Jay returned to the café parking lot just as the mail truck was pulling away. Walking to the mailbox, he noticed that Roland had returned to the catwalk. Maybe he had seen where the guy disappeared so quickly. He would have to ask the ghost later.

He opened the box and scanned the pile left by the mailman. Sticking out from the bottom of the pile was an envelope with no stamp on the corner. Jay carefully pushed the other mail back to look at the unstamped envelope. It had the same red writing on it as the last ransom note.

The guy in the dunes must have been a lookout, and while I was chasing him, his accomplice put this in the mailbox.

Adam pulled up next to Jay.

"Did you see anyone going down the hill when you were driving up?" Jay asked.

"No. What happened?"

"Another envelope," Jay answered, pointing to the mailbox. "And while I was chasing some guy in the dunes, someone else put it in here."

"So, there is more than one person behind this," Adam surmised. "Should have figured."

"Do you have another pair of those gloves?"

"Sure," Adam replied, pulling a pair out of his pocket.

Jay slid the gloves on and grabbed the corner of the envelope. He left the rest of the mail there and headed for his office. Adam shut off his car and followed him into the café.

"Call the sheriff for me, would you?" Jay requested, setting the envelope down on the desk.

He carefully slid the top of the envelope open. Another letter with red lettering, like the last one, was inside. He set it on the desk and unfolded it. Adam walked over to read it when he hung up the phone.

"If you want to see your brother again, leave the necklace, this

Saturday morning by eight a.m. in a plain, brown paper bag in the first row, at the base of the fifth speaker pole at the drive-in. Any sign of the police and Robbie will be returned to you in a body bag," Jay read out loud.

"The drive-in is a wide-open space. Not a very brilliant spot to pick for a drop-off," Adam commented.

"But the first row borders the swamp area to the right and the large treed area behind the screen. To the left is a mobile park. There are many ways to get in and out unnoticed," Jay replied. "And many places to hide once you grab the necklace."

"Another letter?" the sheriff asked as he entered the office. "Let's see it."

"We have a drop-off and a time now. This is what bothers me about this letter. They called him Robbie. They must live here and know that everyone calls him Robbie. Most men with the first name Robert are called Rob or Bobby, not Robbie," the sheriff stated after looking over the ransom note.

"Makes sense, but not necessarily true," Adam agreed. "Anyone hanging around the bar or beach could have heard his name."

"What do you think we should do, Stephen? I hate to use the real necklace, but I don't want to jeopardize Robbie's life either."

"I have never been to this particular drive-in. If we set up that morning before sunrise, are there places to hide around the perimeter to stake out the entire area?" Adam asked.

"Plenty of places. If we put one person under the screen, one near the fence that runs adjacent to the mobile park, two near the snack bar, and one on the marsh side, we should have eyes on the whole area," the sheriff answered. "There are only two ways in and out by vehicle, and we can station men at each opening."

"I think you should plan on using the fake necklace," Adam stated. "Does anyone else know you have a fake?"

"Stella and her gang at the jewelry shop know."

"Do you think they are behind this?" Adam asked.

"Truthfully, I don't think Stella is smart enough, but her sister and whoever the unknown man is might be," the sheriff answered. "I'm in the process of running background checks on all of them."

"We have a few days to firm up this plan," the sheriff stated. "Meanwhile, keep the fake hidden away and don't tell anyone else you have it. If Stella were telling the truth and the necklace was only in the window for ten minutes, not many people would have seen it."

"That doesn't mean that she or her sister didn't run their mouths and tell people about it," Jay replied.

"True, knowing Stella," the sheriff agreed.

"I'm going to run these to the lab," the sheriff said, bagging the letter and envelope. "Hopefully, they will have some answers waiting for me when I get there."

"I'm going to see if I can find Amy. Maybe she learned something from his surfing friends that will help us," Adam said, heading out the door.

Any news on Robbie?

"Not yet, Roland. I noticed that you waited until Adam left before you came to talk to us," the sheriff chuckled.

Don't like strangers...

"Speaking of strangers. The guy you came and warned me about disappeared before I could get to the beach. Did you happen to see where he went when you were standing up in the lighthouse?" Jay asked.

He walked into the sand...

"He what?" the sheriff asked.

"Are there more tunnels out there, Roland?" Jay inquired.

Many more...

"If that is the case, how would our friend know about them unless he was a local?" the sheriff said, confirming his own suspicions.

Many tunnels have been found over the years...

"Are all of them listed in your journal?" Jay asked.

No, I did not find them all. There are many more out there...

"So, someone could have stumbled on a tunnel, and we wouldn't know it," Jay surmised.

Some are better hidden than others, and some reveal themselves with the tides...

"Can you show us the spot where the guy disappeared?' the sheriff asked.

Look under the over-turned dinghy...

"He was hiding under the boat?" the sheriff inquired.

No, look near the boat...in the wall of sand.

"I'll check it out, Stephen, if you want to go to the lab," Jay offered as Roland shimmered out.

"Sounds like a plan. Be careful and keep your cell with you in case you get stuck in one of those tunnels," the sheriff admonished.

I will watch you from my post...

"Thank you, Roland," Jay said, hearing the ghost but not seeing him.

Jay headed for the beach. The sun was shining brightly, and it was surprisingly warm for a day in March. Roland, true to his word, was standing guard on the catwalk watching over his friend. Jay stood next to the abandoned dinghy staring out over the waves.

It was a perfect day for surfing, and he knew if Robbie were home, he would have been out there with Paul riding the waves. He sat down with his back against the boat, closed his eyes, and imagined his brother out on the water. This was the first time since Robbie disappeared that Jay realized he might never see his brother again. He got mad, really mad, and punched the boat over and over again until he looked down and saw blood on his knuckles.

Standing up, he flipped the dinghy over into the surrounding seagrass. As he dug around, nothing unusual appeared, just more seagrass that had been covered by the wind-blown sand. The sand in his split open knuckles stung, but he continued his search.

Jay jumped down onto the beach and looked around at the wall of sand in front of him. The slight breeze was shifting the grains across the front of the dune. Jay noticed that one area of sand wasn't moving as much as the rest. He looked up at Roland, who was shaking his head yes.

Stepping forward, he started to brush the sand away four feet off the ground. Nothing. Jay moved a few feet down and started to brush the sand away again. This time he found rocks. Big rocks that really didn't belong in the middle of a dune. He wondered if it had been part of a seawall that someone erected in the past to protect the coast from erosion.

As he removed more and more sand, the wall of rocks seemed to be contained to one small area, not a large area that a seawall would encompass. The rocks formed a rectangle, three feet tall by three feet wide. As he cleared the sand away, he thought to himself that within a few months or a few more extra high tides, these rocks would have become visible on their own.

The rocks were packed together with a hard mud that had kept them in place. Jay took his pocket knife out of his pocket and started to chip away at one area at the top of the rectangle shape. The filler was fragile, and once Jay got the point of the knife in it, it began to disintegrate because of its age. The first rock came out easily into Jay's waiting hands.

The guy I was chasing didn't escape through here. This hasn't been opened in years.

He shined his flashlight into the small hole and could see a tunnel stretching backward that had been sealed in by the wall. He chipped away around a few more rocks until he could fit his hand into the hole to pull out the rest. The wall crumbled easily once the center rocks were removed. He knelt in the sand and aimed the flashlight beam into the large opening.

It was definitely a tunnel. The walls and ceiling were formed by large wooden beams combined with rocks and the same filler as the door. Jay crawled through the opening and stood up. He cautiously moved forward, checking for signs of a cave-in as he went. The tunnel was as sturdy as the day it was built.

Jay kept walking, not knowing how far in he had gone. He came to a two-way split and stopped to figure out which way to go. He reasoned that taking the right tunnel would lead him in the direction of the café.

This must have been dug from the other direction, and the entrance I uncovered was the end of the digging. The shoreline has been so eroded over the last few hundred years that it ate away the land that extended out to the water.

As he swung the flashlight beam around, he noticed the top of a carving on one of the rocks at the split. Brushing off the years of dust buildup, he found 50R etched into the rock.

That's the first line in Roland's journal clue to the treasure. If I face the rock, is it telling me to take the right tunnel for fifty feet? Why would Roland help me find the treasure after he said he wouldn't? He had to know that the guy didn't come in here, but he sent me here anyway.

Jay swung the beam down into the right tunnel and started to count each step he took. At fifty steps, he stopped and looked around. He saw nothing. A short distance ahead was another split in the tunnel.

Maybe my strides weren't as large as Roland's.

He moved forward to where the next divide in the tunnel was and searched the walls. A small rock that was sitting on the ground propped up against the wall revealed the carving 112L.

I know these are the clues in Roland's journal, but would he make it this easy to find? Besides, he said the clue to finding the treasure is hidden in the pocket watch, and all these directions were in the journal. Maybe he divided the treasure up and hid it in several places, not just one.

Jay decided that he didn't want to go any further without his brother being included in the hunt. He had to go back to the opening and figure out a way to seal it off so that no one else would stumble upon it. Then he had to go to the police station and see if the sheriff got the tox results back yet. He returned the way he came and crawled out of the hole. Pulling the dinghy down off the top of the dune, he centered it over the hole and pushed it into the sand around the hole. It was a perfect fit.

Roland was still watching Jay as he walked back up the beach toward his cottage.

10

Jay arrived at the station and asked to see the sheriff. He was told that he was in his office and to go ahead back. Sheriff Boyd was looking none too happy when Jay rapped on his open door.

"Come on in, Jay," he said, motioning to a chair in front of his desk.

"Is that the lab reports?" Jay asked, taking a seat.

"It sure is," Boyd replied. "It looks like I will have to announce to the local paper after all."

"What's the report say?"

"It seems that the cocktail sauce was laced with LSD. There was also digoxin found in some of the oysters."

"Well, at least we know why the guests were floating around the dance floor and spacing out," Jay stated. "What is digoxin?"

"It's a drug that can make people nauseous and can cause some to have cardiac arrhythmia of the heart."

"And Phil died of a supposed heart attack," Jay mumbled. "Do you think it was Stella and her sister who laced the food?"

"I don't know. It's going to be hard to prove with no body to autopsy," Boyd acknowledged. "The M.E. signed off on the cause of death as natural."

"So, where do we go from here?"

DONNA WALO CLANCY

"I'll call the newspaper and have them send over a couple of reporters. When I give them my statement, I will tell them that it was sabotage, and the café was no way at fault."

"Now more than ever, I think my brother saw whoever did it, and getting the necklace was just an afterthought once they had him tucked away," Jay stated. "He became a way to make a quick buck."

"It makes sense," Boyd agreed. "What are you going to do Saturday morning? Are you going to use the real necklace or the fake one?"

"How well do you think we can cover the area of the drive-in to prevent anyone from escaping once they pick up the necklace?" Jay asked.

"I planned to have six men, myself, and Nickerson on foot located at different points on the property. Two cruisers will be parked up the street behind the buildings in the campground, watching the entrance from both directions."

"What about Adam Cook? Are you going to include him in the operation?"

"No, I am not. He's not part of our regular force," the chief answered.

"Are you still checking on Stella and her sister?"

"I am. Stella was born and raised here, but it seems her sister moved away with the mother when their parents got divorced. Sella chose to stay with her dad here in Anchor Point. What I didn't know was that Stella used to be a jeweler, just like her husband. I haven't figured out why her sister moved back here and ended up staying, though," the sheriff said, pulling out another file folder.

"Who's the guy who was shoveling the walk?"

"He is her sister's boyfriend, John Smith."

"John Smith, seriously? How original," Jay muttered.

"That's his real name, and he has a rap sheet a mile long. We ran a picture I had taken of him outside the jewelry store and sent it through face recognition. He's been in and out of jail since he was eighteen," the sheriff said, giving Jay a copy of the police report.

"All small-time robberies," Jay stated, reading over the report. "Do you think he's capable of murder to get Phil's store?"

"I don't know. We did find out that Stella had two large life insurance policies on her husband totaling a little over a million dollars in payouts. What's more interesting is that Mary has almost identical policies on her brother-in-law taken out a little over a year ago right after she moved here. I have asked the insurance companies to hold off paying the claims until we clear them both of any suspicion."

"They will not be happy when they get that notice," Jay stated, sliding the report back across the desk.

"No, they won't, but I can handle anything they dish out," Boyd said confidently. "It bothers me that they had the body cremated so fast. Last I knew, Phil was going to be buried next to his parents up on the hill. When we would talk at the veteran's hall, he never said anything about his ashes being tossed out over the ocean, only about being buried close to his dad."

"It's obvious that someone didn't want an autopsy done. Who was it, though, Stella or Mary?"

"I'll find out when I go to question them this afternoon. Now that we know what drugs were used and that Phil's doctor confirmed that he took digoxin for his heart, they would have had no problem helping themselves to his medicine."

"Maybe that's what Mary meant when she said to Stella that they have no proof," Jay suggested. "Wouldn't you think they would have figured that the food would have been tested?"

"In all the years I have known her, Stella has never appeared to be too bright," the sheriff admitted. "Maybe it runs in the family."

"I'm going to Robbie's place and see if Amy learned anything out on the beaches, and then I'll be at the café," Jay said, standing up. "I did discover a new tunnel under the point today that I believe is part of Roland's treasure hunt. I didn't pursue it too far as Robbie wants to hunt for the treasure as much as I do."

"We'll find him, Jay."

"Let me know how the newspaper interview goes," Jay requested as he went through the door to leave.

He decided to stop at The Burger Box and get some lunch to go. He knew Susan would fix him something if he asked, but he didn't want to bother her. Maybe he was trying to avoid her. He wasn't sure.

Jay sat on one of the stools at the far corner of the lunch counter while he waited for his to-go order. Loud voices from the opposite corner of the restaurant caught his attention. Sitting in a booth, arguing, was Mary's boyfriend, John Smith, and Greg Peterson.

How the heck do they know each other?

Greg Peterson glanced up and noticed Jay sitting at the counter. A look of panic crossed his face, and he leaned in and said something to his boothmate. They each threw some cash on the table and ran for the door. Jay was going to follow them, but he figured they would go in different directions, and he couldn't follow both at the same time.

I'm sure the sheriff will be interested in what I just saw.

He picked up his lunch and returned to the café, where Susan met Jay at the front door. She had a clipboard in her hand and looked like she had been waiting for his return. Handing it to him, she seemed very confused.

"Did you write this?" she asked.

He glanced at the clipboard and frowned. Across the invoice on the top of the pile were the words NO FAKES in bold red letters.

"No fake what? I don't understand. I order all fresh produce and seafood," Susan asked.

"I didn't write this," he answered. "Where was the clipboard?"

"Hanging on the back wall near the loading dock where all the clipboards are kept. If you didn't write it, who did?"

"I don't know. Was the back door locked?"

"No. It never is on delivery day," Susan replied.

Jay tossed the clipboard on the bench at the front door and ran for the kitchen. The camera that was centered on the back door had black paint sprayed on the lens. He opened the door to check on the cameras on the loading dock. They both had been ripped from their frames and were gone.

"What is going on, Jay?" Susan asked, coming up behind him.

"Whoever has Robbie wrote the message on the clipboard, and they have stolen the café cameras to protect their identities," Jay stated, pointing to the empty spots where the cameras used to be. "This is getting expensive."

"I wish I had paid more attention, but I was busy cooking the sides for tomorrow's lunch," Susan explained.

"I have to go check the security tapes to see if anything was caught to tell us who did this before they sabotaged the cameras," Jay stated, leaving Susan standing there.

He sat at his desk, viewing the recorded films from that morning. A figure dressed all in black with a full ski mask covering his face and head slipped in the back door. This person knew right where the camera was and headed directly to it to spray the lens.

It was a man; Jay was sure of it. In a split second, he was on camera, and Jay could tell he was of medium build and height, but not much more. He wasn't Mary's boyfriend; the figure was too short. He wasn't Greg Peterson; the figure was too well-built. Jay called the sheriff to appraise him of what had happened.

"Jay, do you have a second?" Susan asked, sticking her head in the door.

"Sure, come on in," he answered, without turning away from the screens.

"Did I do something wrong?" Susan asked.

Jay swung his chair around.

"No, why do you ask?"

"Because ever since the Saint Patrick's party, you haven't spoken two words to me," she insisted. "I know you have a lot on your mind with your brother missing, but it's like you are purposely avoiding me. I didn't know if you blamed me for the food being spoiled or not."

"You're right. I do have a lot on my mind, and I am not purposely trying to avoid you. It's just so much is happening, and I can't control any of it. And no, the food was laced with drugs by someone at the party. It wasn't your fault at all."

"I am so glad to hear that. I know that's the attorney side of you coming out wanting to be able to control everything. Still, you can't, and there are plenty of people around you who want to help," Susan replied.

"It's not that I don't appreciate the help, I don't want anyone else to get hurt," Jay admitted. "It really worries me that you were working in

85

the kitchen, unprotected when someone waltzed right in the back door. You could have disappeared to."

"I can protect myself," she insisted. "Can I make a suggestion, though?"

"What?" Jay asked.

"Can we install a bell at the back door that will ring in the kitchen office when there is a delivery out back, or an employee wants to get in for work? That way, we can always keep the door locked," Susan suggested.

"That is a great idea. When I call the security company to get the stolen cameras replaced, I'll see if they can install the bell at the same time," Jay replied. "I think I am going to have them install a couple of extra cameras out in the dock area, but higher up so they can't be reached without standing on a ladder."

"Great! One more thing. I will be leaving a little early today as I have a date tonight. The cooking is almost done for tomorrow, and all I have to do is clean up my workspace," Susan informed her boss.

"You have a date?" Jay asked.

"Yes, I do. Don't look so surprised. I do date you know."

"Anyone I know?" Jay inquired, knowing full well what the answer would be.

"Adam Cook asked me out to dinner, and I said yes. We really haven't progressed in our relationship, so I figured it was time for me to start dating again," she replied.

Jay looked at Susan. He couldn't tell if she was trying to give him an ultimatum or if she was just being truthful with him. She stared right back as if waiting for him to say something.

"Have a great time," was all he could muster.

Jay watched as Susan walked out the door without uttering another word to him. He could tell she was disappointed in his answer, but those old feelings of non-commitment had returned. He had run from his commitment to Cindy, and when he finally told her how he really felt, it was too late. Not knowing if he could go through losing someone again, he wasn't sure if he was relieved or mad that Susan was dating.

She really loves you, you know...

"Oh, hi, Roland. I can't deal with that right now," Jay said, frowning.

You had better, or you might lose her. She is a good woman...

"I know. It's just after losing Cindy…"

Cindy is gone, and Susan is here. If I hadn't been so pigheaded, I might not have died alone...

"Were you dating someone in your time?" Jay asked.

I was courting a beautiful woman named Eliza Nickerson. Smart as a whip she was. Her dad was a sea captain...

"What happened?"

She was offered a teaching job at a private lady's school in Boston. I didn't want to leave my station here on Anchor Point...

"Couldn't you have gotten a job up in Boston? They have lighthouses up there," Jay suggested.

I could have, but I found out that she would have been making a higher pay than I was as a keeper, and I reused to go... Stupid pride, and I lost her...

"She went to Boston without you?"

Aye...

"I'm sorry. You never found anyone else after she left?"

I never looked and spent the rest of my life alone...me and my pipe...

"If Susan wants to date, I can't stand in her way," Jay mumbled.

You're a darn fool...

Jay watched as the angry ghost shimmered out. Roland was right. Jay was making excuses again so he wouldn't have to deal with the issue of commitment. He decided when Robbie was safe at home. He would tell Susan how he felt. Yes, that was just another excuse.

He called the security company and made the arrangements for the new cameras and for the doorbell to be installed at the loading dock door, knowing his employees would have better protection once everything was in place. He glanced through the pile of mail and decided that nothing was so important that it couldn't wait until tomorrow when he returned to work.

Jay walked through the kitchen after making sure the front door was secured. Susan was already gone, and the place was empty. It reminded him of the first day he walked through the café before it opened. A lot had happened since then: good and bad. He locked the back door, set the alarm, and headed for home.

The dogs went crazy as he came through the front door. They had been locked up most of the day and were insistent upon going out. He opened the slider, and they flew through the open door. Pickles stopped to do her thing, but Angie kept running straight ahead toward the dunes.

"Angie! Come!" Jay yelled, but she ignored him.

Then he spotted who she was heading toward. The same person who had been watching the house before was hiding in the tall seagrass at the edge of the first dune. Angie must have been watching him from inside the house, and when she had a chance to go for him, she did. He took off running, Angie on his heels. Jay picked up Pickles and joined in on the chase.

He watched the guy jump down off the edge. Angie had stopped and was barking from the top of the dune. Jay set Pickles down next to Angie and told them both to stay. He jumped down on the beach, and this time, he saw where the guy had hidden himself.

Fifteen feet away, where two dunes met, there was a large enough crevice for the man to hide in without being seen from the beach. Jay cornered him before he could climb up and over the dune to get away. He pulled him out onto the beach and knelt with one knee on his chest to keep him from going anywhere.

"Who are you, and why are you watching my house?" Jay demanded.

Silence. Jay pulled his cell phone out of his back pocket.

"If you don't want to answer me, then you can answer Sheriff Boyd," Jay announced, placing the call.

He pulled the man upright and dragged him up the dune toward the cottage where the sheriff would meet them. The dogs followed, staying close to Jay. The man never looked up or uttered a word as he sat on the steps. Sheriff Boyd arrived and placed the prisoner in the back seat of the cruiser.

"Good luck He hasn't said a word," Jay warned.

"Well, at least we now know that it wasn't John Smith watching the house. Do you have any idea who he is?" Boyd asked.

"I have never seen him before," Jay replied.

"All right. I'll let you know what I find out," Boyd said as he walked around to the driver's side door.

"Come on, girls. Time for supper," Jay announced.

He fed the dogs and pulled his own supper out of the refrigerator. Throwing a cast-iron skillet on the top of the stove, he threw in a chunk of butter and let it heat up. A tossed salad with Russian dressing would accompany his steak. A loud sizzle sounded when the meat hit the hot pan. He stood next to the stove, watching it cook.

"I don't know what to do," he said to the dogs. "Do I take a chance and use the fake necklace on Saturday or not? They warned me not to use it."

He flipped the steak over after seasoning it with salt and pepper.

Is it more important than your brother is?

Jay swung around. Roland was sitting in the captain's chair at the head of the table.

"No, it's not. But, Roland, that's a fourteen-million-dollar necklace. What if they get away with it?"

Does it matter if they return your brother unharmed?

"No, I guess not."

Do you not trust the sheriff enough to protect it?

"I trust him. I'd trust him with my life," Jay replied.

Then why are you worried about using the real one?

"That necklace represents a lot of things I want to accomplish. I want to turn the big building at the back of the café into a bed and breakfast. The smaller building, I intended to turn into a gift shop. That necklace is the security I need for the loans to get these things done," Jay explained. "If they get away with it, that's a lot of year-round jobs that will not become a reality on the Point. And then there is…"

In my day, it was family first. I guess times have changed… then there is what?

Jay put the plate of steak on the table and sat down next to Roland. Roland stared at the food with a real longing in his eyes.

That is one thing I miss… A good piece of meat…

Jay chuckled. He never thought about seeing food around him

constantly but not being able to eat any of it. He wondered how many other things Roland had missed over the last hundred years.

"I have this sinking feeling that even if they get the necklace, it will not save my brother. I think the main reason he went missing was that he witnessed who drugged the food at the party. I don't think they can just let him go as he is a witness to Phil's murder."

He was murdered?

"The sheriff thinks so. Phil had a heart condition and ate oysters that contained digoxin, which could have made his heart beat out of control. But his wife had the body cremated immediately, which is suspicious on its own."

I can see why you are so confused...just know that if they do get the emeralds, my treasure will help with your goals.

"If I ever find it. I don't feel much like hunting for it right now without Robbie. I want to thank you for the clue you showed me."

Roland smiled and shimmered out.

He walked to the fridge and grabbed a beer. Jay ate his supper, sharing the steak with the dogs. He put the dishes in the sink when he was done and grabbed another beer before starting a fire. The two dogs curled up on their beds in front of the hearth, and Jay sat in his recliner, staring into the flames looking for answers to his questions.

11

The café opened on Thursday to an exceedingly small lunch crowd. Kathy, Jay's head hostess, was still in Florida visiting her daughter and would not be back until the following week. The front-page article releasing the sheriff's statement of what had happened at the Saint Patrick's Day party didn't make much of a difference in the café's lunch business. Jay was reading the article at the hostess station when Martha came out of the kitchen.

"Kind of quiet, huh," his mother said.

"It is more than quiet, even for March," Jay replied glumly.

"Don't worry. The sheriff's explanation was in this morning's paper, and that didn't give people a lot of time to read it. We'll be busier tomorrow, you'll see," Martha said, patting her son on the back. "I made two full batches of chowder. That should get us through Sunday."

"Thanks. Mom. You're the best," Jay said, half smiling. "Have you seen Amy today?"

"She was here early this morning when I was making the chowder. Amy said she gong back out on the beaches to talk to more people, and then she was going to start to talk to some of the homeless people that Robbie has helped."

"How much do you know about her?" Jay inquired.

"Not much, really," Martha admitted. "She does seem very concerned about your brother."

"Appearances can be deceiving," Jay mumbled.

"Yes, they can, but her surf friend, Bebee, left to go to California for a surfing competition that they had both signed up for, but Amy stayed here. That has to say something for her character," Martha replied.

"I guess," Jay agreed hesitantly.

"I was here when her friend left. It costs them eight hundred dollars to enter the competition. Bebee was going to try to get Amy's entrance fee back, but there was a no refund clause when they signed up," Martha explained further. "Amy didn't care. She stayed here anyway. And why would she ask her brother to help if she didn't really care for Robbie? I, for one, am going to give her the benefit of the doubt."

"I'm still going to keep an eye on both of them," Jay stated.

"So, I hear Susan went on a date last night with Adam. From what she says, she had a good time," Martha said. "Could there be a little bit of anger or jealousy toward Adam because he asked her out?"

"No. She's free to date who she wants to."

"I don't think you mean that. I sense another commitment issue in the making," Martha replied. "Susan loves you, and you are going to lose her because of your own stubbornness."

"Another unrequested opinion. I wish people would just but out and mind their own business," Jay snapped.

"Fine, I won't bring it up again," Martha said, turning on a dime and returning to the kitchen.

Way to go, Jay, you idiot. She was just trying to help.

The front door opened. The sheriff was fighting to close the door against the wind that had picked up in the last hour.

"So, I hear that this place has the best chowder on the Cape. What are the chances of getting a big old bowl to warm up my insides?" the sheriff requested.

"Hi, Stephen. Go on up to the bar, and I'll bring you some clam chowder. My mom just finished making a fresh batch," Jay replied.

He got one of the waitresses to watch the hostess station and went to

DEATH ON THE HALF SHELL

the kitchen to get the sheriff's chowder. His mother ignored him, but Susan greeted him like she usually did with a big smile.

"Hey, boss, what do you need?" Susan asked.

"I need a bowl of chowder for the sheriff," Jay requested.

"Coming right up," she announced, turning to grab a bowl and filling it out of the steam table. "Anything else?"

"No, that's it. Thanks," he answered, grabbing the bowl and quickly leaving the kitchen.

Jay set the chowder down in front of the sheriff, who immediately leaned in close to the bowl to inhale the delicious smell.

"No one makes chowder better than your mother," he exclaimed, dumping in a package of oyster crackers.

"I assume this isn't just a lunch stop," Jay inquired. "Can I have a root beer, Paul?"

"I'll take one too, please," the sheriff added. "No, it isn't to answer your question. I had an interesting morning at the jewelry store."

"Did you learn anything new?" Jay asked.

"I confirmed my theory that Stella is an airhead. Her sister is a lot smarter than I took her for," the sheriff said in between spoonfuls. "When I requested to talk to her boyfriend, Mary told me he went back to New York two days ago."

"I haven't had a chance to tell you, but I saw John Smith and Greg Peterson having lunch together at The Burger Box yesterday. They were arguing about something, but I couldn't hear what they were saying. That was yesterday, so I guess Mary lied through her teeth about his whereabouts."

"They really don't want me to talk to him, do they?"

"I guess not," Jay agreed. "Did you learn anything else?"

"I got an earful from Mary that the insurance company was holding the payments until the investigation concludes. Stella seemed upset about it, but not as mad as her sister was."

"My first question would be, why did Mary take out insurance policies on Phil in the first place? She's not married to him, and from what I could see, she couldn't stand him," Jay said. "It seems to me that premeditated murder was in the works."

93

"I asked Stella about her background as a jeweler. She admitted that she had gone to gemology school but was nowhere as good as Phil was at cutting gems. She was going to try to keep the jewelry store open but confided in me that her sister was pushing her to sell it and retire."

"So, is she selling it?"

"I can't be sure. Can I get another bowl of chowder?"

"Paul, could you please go get the sheriff another bowl, please? I'll keep an eye on the bar," Jay asked, not wanting to go back to the kitchen if he didn't have to.

"Sure thing. Be right back."

Paul returned, setting the bowl in front of the sheriff.

"So, your life must be quiet now that Bebee has gone to California," Jay commented. "I do appreciate you picking up Robbie's hours until he gets back…if he gets back."

"He'll be back," the sheriff mumbled, giving Jay a look of disgust. "Yea, she was fun to have as a surfing buddy, but not as a girlfriend. She was too high maintenance for my taste. Her brother was just as bad. All they talked about was money and surfing. I work for a living, and she didn't like the fact that I couldn't leave my job and go surfing whenever she wanted me to."

"What was her last name, if you don't mind me asking?" the sheriff inquired.

"Stone. Her family is from California. Her dad is some big wig real estate guy from the Hollywood area. I guess you'd have to have money to travel and surf like they do. I don't think neither her nor her brother have worked a day in their life," Paul replied, tossing a few more packages of oyster crackers next to the sheriff's bowl. "I could never figure out how Amy got hooked up with Bebee. They were nothing alike."

"Do you like Amy?" Jay asked.

"Yea, I do. And I know she really cares for Robbie. Speak of the devil."

Amy walked up to the bar and took the seat next to Jay. She shivered as she removed her coat and hung it over the back of the bar stool.

"Paul, could I have some coffee, please? I am frozen all the way through," she said. "Was my name being tossed around as I approached?"

"You been out on the beaches again?" Paul asked, setting down her coffee.

"Today is the perfect day for surfing. There are a lot of people out on the beach, both surfing and wave watching. No one has heard from or seen Robbie. I'm getting so discouraged," Amy sighed. "Adam's been out talking to the homeless around the point. We were supposed to meet back here for lunch."

"Paul was telling us that Bebee and her brother left for California," Jay offered.

"Thank goodness, yes," Amy replied. "She drove me crazy."

"What do you mean?" the sheriff inquired.

"We didn't have that much in common, except for surfing. I was tired of hearing how much everything costs that they owned," Amy answered honestly.

"How did you meet?" Paul asked while he refilled the two glasses of root beer.

"At the beginning of the summer, when I first met Robbie, I was sitting out on the point waiting for someone with a board, so I had a surfing buddy, you know… protocol and all. Robbie was working and was going to join me after he was done with the liquor order. Bebee and her brother were the first ones to show up, and the three of us hit the waves together. Every time I went surfing, it seemed they were there, too."

"Did Robbie like them?" Jay asked.

"At first he did. Then he got mad at how much they were using us. For two people from a rich family, they never wanted to pitch in for food or beer or anything. We stopped spending time with them and only saw them on the beach. Occasionally they would come to the bar at night for a few hours while Robbie was working."

"They were at the Saint Patrick's Day party," Paul stated.

"They said that was their last chance to say goodbye to everyone before they left. They actually did fork over the money to buy their own tickets for the party," Amy replied. "And now, they have returned to California, probably to hit daddy up for more cash."

"I guess I will add them to my suspect list and check out the California aspect of their story," Sheriff Boyd stated.

"But they are gone," Paul reminded the sheriff. "They had planned to leave well before the party took place."

"It doesn't matter. Now that I have a last name and a location, I can check them out," the sheriff replied, standing up. "How much do I owe you for lunch?"

"It's on the house," Jay answered.

"Thanks! Next time I'll order a lobster roll," his friend joked.

"Then I'll charge you double," Jay retorted.

"I have more digging to do on Stella and her sister. I'll be in touch about Saturday. We need to get to the drive-in before sun-up, probably around five a.m."

"I'll be ready, just let me know," Jay assured him. "I'll walk you to the door."

Out of earshot of anyone else, Jay informed the sheriff that he would be using the real necklace. He couldn't take a chance with his brother's life and would be getting the necklace out of his safety deposit box the following day at nine when the bank opened. He also requested that a plainclothes policeman be stationed outside the bank at that time watching to see if anyone was following him. The sheriff agreed.

Jay returned to the hostess station just as Adam came through the front door to meet his sister. He informed him that he had no luck in locating anyone that had seen Robbie as of late and then went up to the bar to eat lunch with his sister.

No luck?

"No, not yet, Roland," Jay said to the ghost who had appeared behind him

"Oh, my gosh! It's true, George! Look, a real ghost," exclaimed a customer who had come out of the dining room with her husband in tow.

Roland quickly shimmered out.

"I don't see anything," the husband claimed, looking around. "I think you had one too many cocktails at lunch."

"I did not! He was there! I saw him," she insisted as her husband paid the bill.

"Whatever you say, dear," he said, rolling his eyes at Jay and pushing her out the door.

Jay chuckled as he put the bills away in the cash drawer. Sometimes having a ghost on the property could be amusing. Martha came out of the kitchen to tell Jay she was leaving and would not be home until tomorrow night. Her best friend, Theresa, and she were taking a bus trip to Connecticut to play bingo. She was still miffed with her son and offered no hug when she departed.

Martha is not happy with you...

"I know."

What are you going to do to fix it?

"I don't know, Roland, and I can't think about it right now," Jay informed him.

It may already be too late...

Susan walked out of the kitchen, and Roland disappeared. She had her apron off and her purse on her shoulder ready to leave. Jay noticed she was humming and smiling.

"Hey, Boss. It's three, and I'm out of here. Paul is in the kitchen if you need anything," she stated. "Is Adam upstairs yet?"

"Yea, he's eating lunch with his sister," Jay mumbled.

"And me," she smiled, turning around. "Have a great afternoon."

Jay watched Susan walk up the stairs until she was out of sight. Maybe this was the way it was supposed to be. She seemed happy to be dating again. Still staring at the empty stairs, he found himself getting mad. Not at Susan, but at himself. Why did he have so much trouble with commitment?

All these years he kept telling himself it was a guy thing and lots of guys were the same way. When he returned to Anchor Point and reunited with Cindy, he realized this was not the case. It became clear to Jay that he was the problem, and now he was doing the same thing regarding Susan.

She was perfect for him. They shared a love of cooking and the café. She loved dogs even though she was allergic to them. His mother adored her, and so did Roland. Even Robbie had slipped in his two cents here and there in Susan's favor. Everyone could see it but him.

He could see it through, even if his actions said something totally opposite. Maybe it was too soon after losing Cindy. That was just another lame excuse. It was Susan who told him to take his time and make sure the two of them being together was what he wanted. She never pushed him into anything, but she couldn't wait for him forever, either. He knew that.

"Jay. Earth to Jay," Janet said, shoving her purse under the hostess stand. "I'm here. You can leave now."

"Sorry, I was deep in thought," Jay explained. "Thanks for picking up the slack while Kathy is in Florida on vacation. She should be back next week."

No problem," she said, picking up the bottle of cleaning spray and roll of paper towels to wipe down the menu covers. "It's beautiful out when the wind doesn't blow. Have a good afternoon off."

Jay locked the office and went to check with Paul to make sure the bar was covered for the afternoon and evening hours. Out of the corner of his eye, he saw Susan, Adam, and Amy sitting at his favorite table overlooking the water. She was laughing and enjoying herself and hadn't even noticed that Jay was standing at the bar. He stopped in the kitchen to tell the other Paul that he would be at home if he needed Jay for any reason.

He took the dogs out on the Point and let them run. Pickles tried to keep up with her best buddy, Angie, but after a while gave up and ran back to Jay to be picked up and shielded from the wind that was steadily picking up.

It was dead low tide. Jay looked out over the ripples in the sand and the small puddles of remaining saltwater that had got caught in them as the tide went out. Something caught his eye way out on the flats. It almost looked like what was left of the bottom of a ship. He decided to take the dogs inside and go check it out.

He grabbed his camera and changed into his boots. The dogs were happy to be back inside where it was warm. They were busy eating their treats as Jay left. Roland was watching him from the catwalk of the lighthouse as he jumped down on the beach and headed out on the flats.

The wind was whipping the sand against his face as he walked. Jay's eyes were watering, and his face was stinging from the attack. He pulled his coat tighter around him to protect the camera from being sandblasted. The water was up to his ankles when he finally reached the wreck.

It must have become unburied in the last storm.

A good portion of the wooden bottom was buried under the sand. The front section of the keel was fully uncovered and pretty much rotted out. Square-headed rusted spikes were sticking out along the planks that were connected to the keel. Jay estimated that the boat must have been at least sixty feet in length. He also felt that this was only the front section, and the boat must have split in two when it went down.

He took pictures of the wreck from all angles. Jay also took pictures of the shore from where he was standing so that later he could tell where the wreck was situated. One link of a large black chain was sticking out of the sand. Jay pushed the sand aside with his foot, and more links appeared. One of the links had numbers stamped into the iron. He took several pictures hoping maybe it could identify which ship it was or where the chain had been made.

The tide was coming in, and soon the wreck would be underwater. It was getting dark, and Jay realized that he had to get back to shore. Roland was still watching over him as he climbed up the dunes and followed the path through the seagrass to home.

The dogs were sitting at the slider, waiting for him as they could see him when he hit the top of the dunes. Jay was chilled to the bone and shivered as he hung up his coat. He took off his wet boots at the back door and headed straight to the fireplace to start a fire to warm up the cottage.

The dogs ate their supper as Jay waited for a pot of coffee to brew. He wasn't hungry as he had eaten a late lunch at the café, but a cup of steaming hot coffee sounded good. Taking his drink and his camera, Jay stretched out in his recliner in front of the fire.

While letting the hot liquid warm him up from the inside, he scanned the pictures on the digital screen of the camera that he took of the wreck. Seeing several things that interested him, he decided to blow up the pictures and print them so he could see the details better. He would go to the local pharmacy with the memory card in the morning before he went to the bank.

After finishing two cups of coffee, he dozed off in the recliner. Angie was sleeping on her bed at the front of the hearth, and Pickles had jumped up in the chair with Jay. A large bang sounded outside at the front of the cottage. The dogs jumped up and ran to the door barking. Jay grabbed the fire poker and looked out one of the front windows. It was dark, and he couldn't see a thing.

He slid open the bolt lock, flipped on the front porch light, and told the dogs to stay. Cautiously opening the door, he stepped out on the porch and looked around. He closed the door behind him so the dogs couldn't get out to run into the coyotes roaming in the area and walked around the cottage looking for anything or anyone moving.

He approached the far corner of the cottage where his car was parked. There was just enough light so that he could see where the noise had come from and the damage that had been done. Months earlier, someone had trashed his car with spray paint. The same word, murderer, had been painted on the car again. Also, the front windshield had been smashed in.

That must have been the bang we heard.

Feeling like he was being watched, he scanned the area again.

"Who are you? Why are you doing this?" he yelled into the darkness.

The only answer he received was the whistling of the wind through the surrounding seagrass. Deciding not to call the sheriff until the morning, he locked the door and took the dogs upstairs to bed.

Lying in bed, his mind wandered as the picture of his vandalized car kept flashing in his head. All at once, he realized who was doing this to him. His past was coming back to haunt him.

12

Jay was up with the sun. He had gone through two pots of coffee even before he got ready to leave for the bank. Grabbing Robbie's spare set of keys, he would take his brother's jeep and leave his car where it was parked. Too many questions would be raised if Jay drove around in a car with the word murderer painted on it.

At two minutes to nine, Jay pulled up in front of the bank. Out of the corner of his eye, he saw Craig Nickerson sitting in his personal car across the street. The policeman was wearing plain clothes and drinking a cup of coffee. Jay ignored him and walked into the bank. Friday was payday for a lot of people, so the bank was busy. He sat down in a chair and waited his turn to see a customer service representative to get into his box.

He glanced around nonchalantly, looking to see if anyone was around that he did not know or if anyone was watching him. Nothing or no one looked out of place. His name was finally called, and he was escorted into the inner vault. The CSR compared his signature to the signature card on file and unlocked her half of the double lock on the safety deposit box. She left Jay to his business.

Sliding the metal box out of its slot, he lay it on the table and opened it. The real necklace was in a velvet pouch. He set the emeralds on the pouch in the open box. Reaching into the inner pocket of his jacket, he took out the fake necklace and laid it on the table next to the real one. You couldn't tell them apart.

The sheriff was sure whoever showed up to get the necklace would be apprehended. Jay was seriously considering using the fake one instead of the real one. He pulled another velvet pouch out of his coat pocket and slid the fake into it. Putting the real necklace back in the safety deposit box, he had made up his mind what he would do. He would carry out the fake necklace in the pouch and hoped whoever was watching would think he had removed the real necklace from the bank. It was a risky move, but he felt secure in the sheriff's words and promises.

Craig nodded slightly as Jay climbed into the jeep and headed back to his cottage. The cell phone in the center console rang as Jay turned up the hill to home. It was Craig informing him that he sat there for several minutes after Jay left and saw nothing suspicious. Jay thanked him and hung up.

When he arrived home, Amy and her brother were waiting for him on his front steps. He climbed out of the front seat and purposely left the velvet pouch dangling for them to see.

"Let's go inside," Jay requested, stuffing it in his pocket after he made sure they had seen it.

"We came over to see if you knew what happened to Robbie's jeep, but I guess we know the answer now," Adam said. "What happened to your car?"

"A disgruntled employee," Jay answered.

"Wow! Did you call the sheriff?" Adam inquired.

"Not yet, I will."

"Do you think they will let Robbie go after you give them the necklace?" Amy asked as they entered the house. "I'm really getting worried about him. It's been almost a week, and we don't even know how they are treating him. I hope they are at least feeding him."

"I just came from the bank. I am doing everything I can to do what they have requested to get my brother back. Do you want to see it?" Jay asked, placing his hand over his pocket.

"May we?" Amy replied hesitantly.

"Follow me," Jay instructed, leading the pair to the kitchen table.

He removed the pouch from his pocket. He carefully laid the velvet pouch on the table. He removed the necklace, handling it like it was worth fourteen million dollars. Holding it up, he angled it to reflect the morning sun coming in the window over the sink.

"Oh, Jay, it's beautiful," Amy whispered. "May I?"

Jay handed the necklace to Amy. She held it up against her neck and smiled broadly.

"How do I look?"

"Stunning," her brother answered, laughing. "Too bad you're not royalty. You look good covered in priceless gems."

"I do, don't I?" she replied. "I might look good, but I'd be a physical wreck owning this thing. Too much can go wrong when you have money. A prime example is Robbie being kidnapped. I'd rather be comfortable and happy than rich and wary of everyone."

"Truer words were never spoken," Jay agreed, trying to figure out if she was being truthful or just putting on a show for him.

"Do you need any help tomorrow morning with the stake-out?" Adam asked.

"You'll have to talk to the sheriff. I don't think he was going to include you because you are not one of his regular officers and not covered by their insurance," Jay stated.

"I understand," Adam relented.

"I hope you get them," Amy said, setting the necklace gingerly down on the velvet pouch. "I have this gut feeling that Robbie is somewhere close by. I don't know why, but I just do."

"Hopefully, he'll be home tomorrow," Jay stated, putting the necklace back inside the pouch. "Now, if you'll excuse me, I have to get to the café."

"We'll be at Robbie's. Please let us know what happens," Amy requested. "Right now, I'm going back out on the beaches to see if anyone different is around that I haven't talked to yet."

"I'll be in touch when I know anything," Jay said, opening the front door.

Jay waited until they were a reasonable distance away from the cottage before he opened the wall safe to put the necklace away. Even though it was a fake, it was still worth a few grand and should be protected for its use in the morning.

Tomorrow morning...

Roland was standing next to the fireplace when Jay turned around. Pickles was sitting at his feet, tail swishing back and forth.

"I guess Pickles has accepted you," Jay smiled. "I don't think she quite understands that you can't pat her or toss the ball for her."

Who says I can't?

The little red ball that was sitting next to the dog suddenly rolled across the room. Pickles ran after it and returned it to the ghost.

Only once, my little friend...

"No more, Pickles. Go play with Angie," Jay instructed the dog.

Will Robbie be home soon?

"I sure hope so, Roland. The sheriff has everything planned for the exchange. If he's right, we should have someone in custody tomorrow morning that can tell us where Robbie is hidden."

Real or fake?

"I have the fake one, but I planted the idea that I went to the bank to get the real one," Jay told him. "I fought with which one to use, but the sheriff insists that it won't get to the point where the suspect even gets to open the bag before he is grabbed."

I hope he is right.

"I don't think I'll get much sleep tonight. We are to meet behind the variety store across the street from the drive-in at four-thirty a.m. to firm up plans. At seven-forty-five, I will drive in and drop off the necklace and then leave again. After that, it up to the sheriff and his men."

I will be waiting... with Martha.

"You two will be the first to know," Jay assured him. "Now, I have to go to the café and get ready for the lunch rush, if you can even call it that."

Things will get better, wait, and see.

"Come on girls! Let's go to the café," Jay said to the dogs as Roland shimmered out.

Lunch was a bit busier than the previous day. The newspaper got the word out that the café was not to blame, and the sheriff assured the locals he would find out who sabotaged the Saint Patrick's Day party. As the customers returned for their bowls of hot clam chowder on a cold day, they told Jay they were glad to be back. Lunchtime went by fast, and it was three o'clock before Jay knew it.

One of his part-time employees took over the front desk, and Jay was free to go. He walked upstairs to the bar. There were a few patrons left eating at the tables near the panoramic windows and two sitting at the bar enjoying a liquid lunch.

"Can I have a beer, Paul?" he requested, sitting at the end of the bar that his brother always covered when he was working.

He took a slug of beer and walked around to the backside of the bar. Standing where his brother would stand while serving drinks, he gazed around the area to see where Robbie could see when working, which was basically the whole room. Where the banquet tables had been placed the night of the party, as well as the area around the elevator where the food was brought up from the kitchen, were in plain sight from Robbie's work area.

The crowd of people that night would have made it a lot harder to see the banquet tables. Still, very few people would have been in the back area except for the employees who were restocking the buffet. Anyone who didn't work here would have stuck out, and Robbie would have noticed them.

"You okay, Jay?" Paul asked, reaching around him for a particular type of whiskey.

"Yea, I'm just trying to see what Robbie might have seen the night of the party," he replied. "Paul, how long have you and my brother been friends?"

"Am I on the suspect list now?" he asked, returning the bottle of whiskey to its spot.

"No, I just was trying to figure out if I was the only one who didn't know what he was doing for the homeless on the Point. Me and my mom, that is."

"Robbie and I have been best buds since fifth grade. My family used to vacation here in the summer and moved here permanently at the end of my fourth-grade school year. I remember meeting your brother out on the beach about two weeks before school was starting, and we discovered we were in the same homeroom. He talked to me when no one else did. As far as him helping the homeless, he's been doing that since our junior year in high school."

"I never realized…" Jay muttered.

"He didn't want people to know. Only the ones that helped him to take care of the people he was concerned for," Paul stated, wiping down the bar. "Your brother has one huge heart. He does without so others don't have to."

"I'm finding that out."

"When Robbie and I have the same shift, we divide our tips three ways," Paul said, pulling a big plastic water bottle out from under the bar that contained money. "The third portion is put into this jug. We saved it up all summer for Robbie to use during the winter to pay off the homeless bills that he occurs."

"That's awesome. Does Amy help out at all?"

"She has been right at Robbie's side when he goes out in a storm to look for the homeless to try to talk them into going to the shelter."

"She doesn't work, does she?" Jay inquired.

"As soon as Amy decided to stay here with Robbie, she started looking for work, but you know how hard it is in the off-season to get a job on the Point. Last I knew Robbie was going to talk to you about her getting a job in the kitchen. She loves to cook, and I think she would be a great asset to Susan," Paul replied honestly.

"It sounds like they are close."

"Really close. I wouldn't be surprised if she's the one that your brother will marry…if he comes home," Paul added quietly.

"He'll make it home. And when you see Amy tell her she has a job as a prep cook whenever she wants to start," Jay said, downing the rest of his beer and setting the bottle in the return rack. "If you need me, I'll be at home."

The dogs had to be put on their leashes for the walk home. It was dusk, and Jay wasn't exactly sure when the coyotes would come out on their nightly hunt for food. As they approached the cottage, Angie stopped dead in her tracks and started growling. Jay looked in the area where she was staring and saw a man standing there watching them.

"Who are you?' Jay yelled.

No answer.

Jay advanced with the dogs leading the way. The man looked vaguely familiar to Jay, and when they got within twenty feet of him, he simply disappeared. Angie stopped growling the second he was gone.

"Great! Just what we need, another ghost on the Point," Jay said to the dogs as he turned them around to head back to the cottage. "But why did he look so familiar?"

Jay had brought home a slab of swordfish from the café for supper. He broiled it with fresh lemon juice, butter, and thyme. A Caesar salad and his favorite beer completed the menu. The trio finished supper and retired early as Jay had to be up early.

He tossed and turned all night. Jay couldn't help but wonder if he had made the correct decision in using the fake necklace, but there was nothing he could do to change it now. The bank didn't open until nine, and the drop-off was at eight. Not sleeping a wink, he got out of bed at four o'clock and showered. While the coffee brewed, he took the dogs out, staying close to the back deck.

A little before five, he pulled into the back parking lot behind the variety store across the street from the drive-in. He tucked Robbie's jeep as close as he could to the building so it could not be seen from the road. Minutes later, the sheriff and Nickerson pulled in with no lights on and parked next to the jeep.

"Where's your car?" the sheriff asked Jay.

"Long story. I'll tell you later," Jay informed him.

"Bailey, are you in place?" the sheriff asked into his shoulder radio.

"Yes, sir."

"Pratt?"

"Yes, sir."

A second cruiser pulled up, and three more police dressed in black from head to toe climbed out. The fourth drove the cruiser away once everyone exited. They all gathered around the sheriff.

"You have each been given your position in the drive-in. Stay low to the ground and quiet. Keep your radios on low and check in every hour or if you see any movement. Jay will arrive at seven forty-five, drop off the package at the speaker in the first row, and then leave. Everyone understand?" Sheriff Boyd asked.

A mumble of yesses sounded.

"We will cross the road, one man at a time, and take our places. Fulton, you're first," Boyd instructed. "No lights, night goggles only."

"I'll be at home until seven-thirty," Jay stated, feeling better once he saw the plan in action.

"Just remember, Jay. Drop of the necklace and then leave. If you hang around, the plan might fall apart," Boyd cautioned.

"I will. I'll be at the convenience store a mile away. Just call me," he replied as he climbed into the jeep.

Sitting at home, Jay managed to drink another full pot of coffee while watching the clock. It was too early even for the dogs who snuggled together on the dog bed under the kitchen table. The velvet pouch with the fake necklace sat on the table in front of him. Jay was not one to pray, but he closed his eyes and mumbled a small prayer that he would see his brother today.

I'll say one, too.

"Thank you, Roland. Right now, every little bit helps."

A new spirit. I saw him yesterday.

"Do you know who he is?' Jay asked.

No. He is of your time, not mine.

"I saw him last night. He looked familiar to me, but I couldn't place who he was," Jay admitted. "If you see him again, please keep an eye on him."

I will. You bring Robbie home. Martha cries every night for her son.

"We are going to do our best. It's time for me to go deliver the necklace," Jay said, standing up and grabbing the pouch. "Girls be good."

I'll be waiting.

The colors of dawn were still looming in the sky when Jay drove into the drive-in entrance. He parked at the end of the first row, picked up the necklace that was on the seat next to him, and put it in the brown paper bag like requested. Walking to the third speaker, he set the paper bag at the base of the speaker and walked back to the jeep. He drove away without looking back, knowing the sheriff and his men were in place.

Jay pulled into the convenience store and went in for more coffee. One of the sheriff's men, Tim Breen, was sitting at the counter having breakfast. Jay sat with him so Tim could relay what was being said in his earphone.

"A car is pulling in, but it's stopped up near the entrance," Tim told Jay. "They can't see who is in the car yet."

Jay sat in silence, his stomach churning from all the coffee he had consumed since he woke up.

"The car has pulled into the fourth row, far end, and stopped. There are two people in the car, and they are looking around. A male and a female are sitting in the front seat," Tim relayed to Jay. "The man is pointing toward the speaker where the necklace is sitting."

"Do they know who they are?" Jay inquired.

"They haven't said. The female is getting out of the car and moving to the driver's seat. The male suspect is walking to the front of the field. He's looking around as he walks," Tim said. "Wait a minute. He turned around and is heading back to the car. They are moving in. Come on."

"I'll ride with you," Jay announced.

They raced into the drive-in and stopped a row away from where the police had a car surrounded. Jay moved forward, hoping to hear what was being said but was cautioned to stay back.

"We didn't do anything," Jay could hear the man protesting from the side of the car. "We were told it would be okay for us to come in here and let my daughter practice her driving."

"Who told you it was okay?"

"A young girl that we met at The Clam Shack when we were having lunch there. She overheard us talking about my daughter just getting her permit and suggested this place. She told us that Saturday morning would be a good time as no one would be here."

"A young girl?" the sheriff asked.

"That's her!" he exclaimed, pointing behind the sheriff toward the big screen.

Adam Cook was walking toward the group holding a young woman by the arm and the velvet pouch, on the other hand. She was squirming, doing her best to break free from his grasp.

"Here's your kidnapper," Adam announced, handing the sheriff the necklace. "When you ran for the car, she came out of the woods and grabbed the bag."

"Beebee! I thought you left for California," Jay stated, stepping forward. "Where's my brother?"

"This is Amy's friend, Beebee?" the sheriff inquired.

"Yes, it is. I'm not going to ask again. Where is my brother?" Jay asked through clenched teeth.

"I have no idea," she answered, rolling her eyes.

"What do you mean, you have no idea? You had better start talking. You are in serious trouble," the sheriff warned.

"Nothing my rich daddy can't fix," she answered flippantly.

"All your father's money can't fix kidnapping charges," the sheriff stated, frustrated with the young girl's air of privilege.

"I told you. We didn't kidnap Robbie."

"We?" Jay asked.

"Oh, I guess I shouldn't have said that," she mumbled, twirling a strand of her hair around her finger.

"Fan out and see if you can find anyone else in the area," the sheriff ordered. "Sir, you and your daughter are free to go. We are sorry for the scare we put you through. Before you go, can you please give my deputy your name and where you are staying so we can get a statement from you later today?"

"Sure. I hope you find who you are looking for," he replied, glaring at Beebee. "I don't appreciate being used to commit a crime."

"Peterson, handcuff her and bring her to the station. Put her in holding tank one until I get there," the sheriff ordered.

When the cruiser left, Sheriff Boyd turned to Adam Cook.

"It's not that I don't appreciate the help, but what are you doing here?"

"I figured that another set of eyes couldn't hurt," Adam answered. "I'm sorry if I overstepped my bounds. Do you think she was telling the truth about not kidnapping Robbie?"

"I don't know. I need to go back to the station and question her some more before she calls her father or one of his attorney's and clams up. She doesn't appear to be overly bright and might make a mistake and say something that might help us to find him."

"I'll stick around here and look for her brother," Adam offered. "I mean, if that's okay with you, sheriff."

"Fine, but if you find anyone, call one of my officers. I want everything on the up and up when we make arrests," the sheriff instructed. "Jay, do you want a ride back to the convenience store to pick up your vehicle?"

"Yea, and do you mind if I follow you to the station and listen in when you question Beebee?"

"As long as you agree to stay behind the observation glass and not interrupt the interrogation," Boyd stated.

"I just want to find my brother, and I'll do whatever that takes," Jay agreed, climbing into the cruiser. "How long will you have to keep the fake necklace as evidence?"

"It all depends on the girl's father and his attorneys. Why?"

"I need it for the opening of the Tunnel of Ships in April," Jay answered.

"I'll do my best to get it back to you by then," the sheriff said, pulling into the convenience store parking lot. "See you at the station."

Jay climbed into his brother's jeep and sat there as the morning sun, thinking.

If Beebee is telling the truth, then who still has my brother? It must go back to the Saint Patrick's Day party. Robbie had to have seen who tainted the food, and whoever it was, was scared that he would identify them.

Jay put the jeep in gear and headed into town. Main Street was extremely busy for a winter day in March. As he drove by the Anchor

Point Jewelry Store, he noticed the abnormally large number of customers that were shopping there.

I'll have to check that out when I'm done at the police station.

Jay entered the station and was told the sheriff was in interrogation room A. Entering the adjoining room, he stood behind the two-way mirror watching the events of the room.

"Switch this on, and you can hear what's being said," Nickerson said, reaching over Jay's shoulder and flipping a toggle switch into an up position.

"Who are you working with?" Jay heard the sheriff say.

Silence.

"Where is Robbie being held?"

"I told you before, we didn't kidnap Robbie," she snarled. "We only wanted the necklace so we could sell it for the money. My brother said he was approached by some guy that said he had connections and could sell it for us."

"You expect me to believe that? Your family is very well to do. You don't need money," the sheriff shot back.

"My daddy is very well to do, but he doesn't share," Beebee claimed. "My brother and I have to beg for every cent we get from the old tightwad."

"Did you ever hear of getting a job?"

"I don't want to have to work," she whined. "I want to travel and surf. My mother has never worked a day in her life, and I intend to be just like her."

The sheriff's head turned as the door to the interrogation room opened. Deputy Nickerson entered the room, whispered something in the sheriff's ear, and left again.

"It seems we caught your brother running from the drive-in and into the trailer park, and we'll be questioning him next," the sheriff explained, hoping for a reaction.

As Beebee opened her mouth to say something, the door opened a second time, and an older gentleman in a fancy three-piece suit entered the room and planted his briefcase on the table between the sheriff and the young girl.

"My client will not be answering any more questions until I have had time to confer with her," the man announced loudly. "And that goes for her brother also."

The sheriff closed the file in front of him and stood up.

"My deputy will be stationed outside the door. Your clients are under arrest and will be spending the weekend in our jail until bail can be set on Monday," he announced as he left the room.

Jay exited the adjoining room as the sheriff walked past.

"How do these attorneys get here so fast? That never ceases to amaze me," he complained, shaking his head and slamming the file against his leg.

"Nickerson said that the brother called the attorney when he saw his sister get caught picking up the necklace, and then he made a run for it."

"They must have them on speed dial," the sheriff grumbled.

"Some of my clients did, I can't lie," Jay admitted, following the sheriff to his office.

"Well, we are no closer to finding your brother than we were this morning," Boyd said, plopping himself in his chair. "I can't help but feel we are missing something."

"I keep going back to the party. It bothers me that Phil was the only one that died from the tainted food. I'm sure Robbie saw what happened and they had to silence him. I just hope they didn't silence him permanently. Can I look over the lab reports?"

"Sure," the sheriff said, throwing the file his way. "The crime scene photos are in there, too."

"What are these?" Jay asked, holding up an envelope full of pictures.

"I just received those today and haven't had a chance to look through them. The manager for the band that Robbie hired took pictures of the event all night. He uses them for promotional purposes. I asked him to send me a set," the sheriff replied.

"There's got to be two hundred pictures here," Jay noticed.

"Two sets of eyes are better than one. Give me half the pile, and we'll go through them right now," the sheriff suggested.

The two men sat quietly sifting through the pictures. The sheriff took a magnifying glass out of his top drawer and set it on the desk for the men to use to scrutinize the pictures closer. Jay looked at one picture of the bar area and put it down. Something caught his eye, and he picked it back up. Using the magnifying glass to make sure he saw what he thought he did, he stood up and passed the picture to the sheriff.

"Do you see what I see? I know who has Robbie," he announced.

13

"I never would have suspected him, never in a million years. I should have known the others weren't smart enough to plan something like this," the sheriff exclaimed. "Nickerson, grab a few of your men and get in here."

"I never even saw him at the party," Jay mumbled.

The sheriff outlined what he wanted each man to do. They had to round up all the suspects at the same time so that none of them would have a chance to get to where Robbie was being held captive and disposed of. They would meet back at the station when all the suspects were in custody.

"Jay you come with me. Fulton you, too," the sheriff ordered. "It may take three of us to get him into custody."

Two cruisers were dispatched to one location, another to a second location, and the sheriff's cruiser to another. The anger inside Jay was rising with each passing minute. How could he have been taken in so easily? They rode up the hill to the lighthouse and parked in front of Jay's cottage. Roland was watching them from the catwalk and paced back and forth as the three men made their way to Robbie's cottage.

"Stand to the back, Jay," the sheriff ordered as he knocked on the door.

Amy answered the door.

"Where is your brother?" the sheriff inquired.

"He left early this morning and hasn't come back yet," she replied, looking past the sheriff to see the others standing there. "Why? What's going on?"

"Do you know where he is?"

"No, I don't. Jay, what is going on? Why do you want to find my brother?" Amy asked again.

"You need to come to the station with us," the sheriff informed her, side-stepping an answer.

"Okay, let me get my purse," Amy stammered.

He's watching you from behind the first dune.

"Thanks, Roland," Jay yelled, running in the direction of the beach.

Jay arrived at the area Roland had directed him to, but Adam Cook was nowhere to be seen. The sheriff caught up with him, and they both scoured the area for any sign of where the suspect went.

He's hiding in the old maintenance building.

Their suspect was watching from just inside the door where he saw the two men approaching. He took off for the road that led down the hill into town, but Jay was faster, and he tackled him before he reached the bottom of the hill. Cook was strong and managed to free one arm to punch Jay in the gut. It knocked the wind out of Jay, and he let go of Cook, but the sheriff caught up just in time to pounce on the suspect and pin him to the ground.

"Where's my brother?" Jay demanded as the sheriff cuffed his prisoner.

He has Robbie?

"Yes, he does, Roland. And if I have to beat him within an inch of his life, he's going to tell me where he is," Jay growled.

They walked their prisoner back to the cruiser, where his sister and Deputy Fulton were waiting.

"Adam, why are you handcuffed? What did you do?" Amy pleaded.

Her brother growled something under his breath as he was put in the back seat of the cruiser. Amy looked devastated and bewildered as the sheriff turned to her next.

"Amy, please ride with Jay to the station. Everything will be explained there," the sheriff requested.

A voice came through the sheriff's shoulder radio, telling him that the other four suspects had been rounded up and were at the station in the holding tanks.

"Let's go find out where your brother is," the sheriff said to Jay.

They met back at the station. Cook was put in a separate holding cell away from the other suspects. Amy and Jay were concealed in an observation room off interrogation room 1, waiting for the questioning to begin.

"You really like my brother, don't you?" Jay asked Amy.

"No, I really love your brother, and he loves me. Your brother is a one of a kind human being. He has so much compassion for others, and that's why I love him. I hope you don't think I know anything about what is going on here. My heart has been broken worrying about Robbie," Amy answered. "I can't believe my brother had anything to do with his kidnapping. Why would he?"

"Let's just wait and see what is said," Jay replied.

The first suspect was ushered into the interrogation room. Adam Cook was seated, and the questioning began. Amy started sobbing, thinking that her brother could even be involved in this whole mess.

"Where is Robbie?" the sheriff demanded.

Adam Cook glared at him but didn't utter a word.

"You have nothing on me," he finally stated after a long silence.

"Oh, but we do," the sheriff said, throwing a picture down on the table in front of him. "Care to explain this?"

Cook glanced at the picture set in front of him.

"I bet this is something you didn't plan on. The band manager was taking pictures all night and caught you standing near the elevators on film. And what is that item you are holding in your hand?"

"I want an attorney," he growled.

"I believe that is Robbie's green sequin hat that you have hold of," the sheriff continued. "Care to explain how it came to be in your possession, and then how it ended up on the floor at the loading dock door?"

"I want an attorney," Cook repeated.

"That's fine. We have your other partners in custody, and they are not as stoic as you are. When we get around to questioning them, I am sure they will throw you under the bus in due time," the sheriff replied, picking up the picture and tucking it in his shirt pocket.

The door flew open, slamming against the wall with a loud bang. Amy stood there, tears streaming down her face.

"Sorry, chief, she got by me before I could stop her," Fulton apologized.

"Where is Robbie?" she demanded through gritted teeth.

"Amy…"

"Don't you Amy me. Where is my boyfriend? How dare you come here on the pretense of helping me to find him and all the while lying to my face. What kind of brother are you?"

"A brother who is sick and tired of watching Dad suffer. You don't see it because you are never around,' he screamed back at her. "Uncle Phil promised to help Dad, and he didn't."

"So, you got even with him by killing him? What happened, did Robbie see what you were doing, and you had to keep him quiet?"

"It started out that way. We…" Cook admitted out of anger. "I'm not saying anymore without an attorney. I've already said too much."

"We? Who is 'we'?" Amy inquired.

"I love you, Amy, but I am not saying anything else," her brother answered.

"Fulton take Mr. Cook to make his one phone call and then lock him up," the sheriff directed.

"And I don't know where Robbie is," Cook shouted to his sister as he was led away by the deputy. "I really don't."

"Miss Cook, you have to assure me you will stay in the observation room and not interfere again. If you can't, I will have to insist that you leave," the sheriff admonished.

"I apologize. I am still in shock that my brother had something to do with Robbie's kidnapping and Uncle Phil's death. May I see what the picture was that you showed my brother?" Amy requested.

The sheriff handed her the picture, and her face lit up.

"I know this man. His name is John Smith. I thought Adam was joking, but he wasn't as that was his real name. He came to the cottage a couple of times. My brother told me he arrested Smith when he was tied to another case that Adam was working. Smith used to be a fence and spent time in jail when he got caught committing a jewelry heist," Amy offered.

"We have already obtained his police record, but thank you," the sheriff said. "That does solidify the fact that they know each other, though."

"I won't interrupt you again," Amy promised the sheriff, heading back into the observation room with Jay.

"Bring out Stella Cook," the sheriff yelled to his deputy.

Stella sat at the table, hands folded, looking like she was ready to burst into tears at any moment. As nasty as she had been to Jay at the jewelry store, he felt bad for her at this moment.

"Stella, do you know why you are here?"

"I'm not sure, but my sister said I should not talk to you until our attorney gets here," she answered. "I don't understand why I need an attorney. I didn't do anything."

"You do know that Phil's death was not an accident? He was murdered," the sheriff inquired.

"Phil died of a heart attack. That's what my sister said the doctor told her," Stella claimed.

"You didn't talk to the doctor yourself?"

"No, I was too upset at Phil's death to deal with doctors. My sister volunteered to take care of everything for me, even the arrangements."

"She was the one who had Phil cremated?"

"Yes, she had me sign papers. Mary said they were for paying the funeral home bills, not for cremating him. It was already done before I realized what had happened," Stella sobbed. "Mary told me that Phil told her he wanted his ashes scattered out over the ocean. He always told me he wanted to be buried next to his dad."

"Why were you so nasty to Jay at your store the day we came to pick up the necklace?" the sheriff asked.

"Mary told me that Jay was going to try to take my husband's business away from me," Stella answered.

"And why would he do that?"

"Because that what he did to the Petersons. He took all their dad's money away from them. He's an attorney and knows his way around the law to take things from people."

The sheriff glanced at the two-way mirror.

"Were the Peterson's interested in your store?" the sheriff asked.

"Greg Peterson has always wanted to buy the property. He wanted the Main Street location to open his own place, but my Phil would never sell it to him."

"Were you going to sell it to him?"

"At first I wasn't going to. I wanted to downsize the jewelry store and keep it open. I am a jeweler in my own right. That's how Phil and I met. But my sister talked me into selling it to Greg Peterson and retiring," Stella admitted.

"Did you have an insurance policy on your husband," the sheriff asked, testing Stella honesty.

"Yes, we each had one on each other in case something happened, and the other one could continue with life without worrying about finances."

"Did you know that Mary had taken out a million-dollar policy on Phil?" the sheriff asked, watching for her reaction.

"Why would she do that? He wasn't her husband," Stella replied, eyes wide.

"Do you know that your sister was working with others to murder your husband, collect the insurance, and talk you into selling the store?"

Stella sat there, staring at the sheriff, not liking what she was hearing.

"Stella, have you done an inventory on the jewelry store in the last few weeks?"

"Mary and John did the inventory."

"How convenient. I wonder how much is missing that they have sold off under your nose. John Smith is a fence and has lots of connections to sell stolen gems," the sheriff replied, finding it hard to believe that Stella could be this gullible.

"I did notice several things missing, but my sister assured me that they were rotating the stock so customers could see different pieces when they shopped. She said the missing items were locked in the safe, and I never thought anything about her answer. I trusted my sister," Stella said, going from meek to mad in a quick moment as she was now starting to understand that she was had by her own family.

"Do you know where Robbie is?"

"Oh, please don't tell me that they had something to do with Robbie disappearing."

"We believe they did. One of them knows where Robbie is being kept," the sheriff informed her.

"I think I am going to be sick," Stella said, gripping her stomach.

The sheriff retrieved a metal wastebasket from the corner of the room and set it next to Stella. She grabbed it just in time.

"I'll go get you some wet paper towels," the sheriff offered, not wanting to watch her vomit.

He stepped into the observation room and motioned to Jay to step out in the hallway.

"What do you think? Is Stella in on it?"

"I don't think she is," Jay answered. "I think she's as innocent as Phil was."

"I'll give her time to compose herself and return her to her cell. I'm not ready to let her go just yet," the sheriff admitted. "I want to keep the two sisters apart for now."

"Good idea. Mary may try to tell Stella what to say," Jay agreed.

"I had Nickerson pick up Greg Peterson and bring him in for questioning. He's up next."

The sheriff waited with Amy and Jay behind the two-way mirror while Stella was ushered out, and Greg Peterson was brought in. The sheriff entered the room and seated himself opposite the suspect. Staring at Greg and not saying anything, the sheriff waited to see if he would break and say something first. It worked.

"Why am I here?" Greg demanded.

"Are you trying to buy Anchor Point Jewelers?"

"Yes, that's no secret. I have wanted to buy that property for years."

"But you had to wait for Phil to die to get it," the sheriff stated.

"I didn't go to them; they came to me."

"Who's they?"

"Mary and John," he replied.

"You didn't think it was funny that they came to you and not Stella?"

"Mary said she was handling all the financial affairs for her sister after she fell apart because of her husband's death. Some people can't handle death well, and I didn't think anything of it when Mary told me that."

"Do you also know that Phil was murdered so they could talk Stella into selling the place to you?"

"Wait a minute! I don't know anything about murder. A guy named Cook came to me and asked if I was still interested in buying Phil's place. I said yes, and he said he'd get back to me. I thought Phil died of a heart attack."

"He did. But it was caused by a drug overdose of digoxin that was fed to him on purpose to speed up his heart. Just how bad did you want his property?" the sheriff questioned.

"Not that bad," Greg stated emphatically.

"So, you are telling me that you know nothing about the murder plan or Robbie's kidnapping?"

"That's what I'm telling you. I may despise Jay Hallett for taking my dad's money, and I might act like a jerk sometimes. Still, I would never do anything to hurt his family, especially Robbie. I really respect him, and my mom used to go to bingo with Martha. Robbie is looked up to in this community, and I would never do anything, I repeat anything, to hurt him," Greg insisted. "I just wanted to buy Phil's building, that's all."

"Stay here," the sheriff said, leaving the room and going to talk to Jay.

"I don't think he had anything to do with what happened," he said to Jay.

"I don't think so either. He was just a way to make more money for Mary and her crew to steal. I bet that if the building were sold, Mary would have told Stella a different price than what it was actually sold for. She would have pocketed a hefty balance of the money."

"Well, that leaves John Smith and Mary. I bet they both know where Robbie is. Let's see who we can get to break first," the sheriff announced. "John Smith has nothing to lose by cutting a deal with us. He broke his parole and is definitely going back to jail, but let's see for how long this time."

John Smith was escorted into the interview room. He looked none too happy as he squirmed in his chair. The sheriff sat down opposite him and didn't say anything. He just let him squirm a little more and sweat a little more. Finally, the sheriff spoke.

"Where is Robbie Hallett?"

"I don't know anyone by that name," Smith mumbled, fidgeting with the ring on his hand.

"Nice ring. "Did you steal it from Phil's store?" the sheriff asked.

"I didn't steal it! Mary gave it to me," he answered angrily.

"So, Mary stole it?"

"I don't know, I didn't ask," he mumbled, settling done again.

"You are going away for a long time this time. I doubt you will ever see the light of day again after you are charged with this murder and kidnapping charge," the sheriff stated.

"Murder! I didn't murder anyone. What are you talking about?" Smith claimed, jumping up out of his chair. "I may be a thief, but I am no murderer."

"You didn't help to kill Phil Cook?"

"He died of a heart attack. That's what Mary told me."

"That's what she wanted it to look like," the sheriff replied.

Smith remained silent as if processing all the information that he had just received. He frowned when he realized that Mary had used him, and he wasn't a happy person.

"What do you want to know?"

"Where is Robbie Hallett for starters?" the sheriff repeated.

"If I cooperate, can I get a deal?" Smith asked, before admitting to anything.

"We'll see how important your information is," the sheriff answered.

Jay and Amy were watching through the window, both hopeful they would finally find out where Robbie was.

"This looks like it's going to take a while. I'm going to use the ladies'

DONNA WALO CLANCY

room. I'll be right back," Amy stated. "Do you want a coffee out of the machine?"

"I'll be here," Jay answered, listening to the sheriff more than Amy.

"Where is Robbie?" the sheriff continued.

"I don't know exactly, but I do know who does know," he replied.

"Is it Mary?"

"No, she's not smart enough to pull off something like this. She just saw an opportunity to pocket some money and joined in on the plan," Smith said. "What about my deal?"

"No deal until I get answers. Who put the drugs in Phil's food?"

"Little Miss Innocent sitting at the bar. She waited until Phil set down his plate to take a drink of his beer and bam," Smith stated. "She had full run of the place dating Robbie and laced all the other food with drugs before the party even started."

"Are you saying that Amy Cook overdosed her uncle and laced the rest of the food?" the sheriff asked in disbelief.

"That's exactly what I am saying."

Jay jumped up and flew out into the hall. There was no sign of Amy anywhere. He asked the deputies at the front desk, and they confirmed that she had left just minutes before. The sheriff met up with Jay on his way back to the observation room.

"Where is she?"

"Gone. She said she had to use the bathroom right before Smith announced her name. We need to talk to Adam Cook again. He must know where my brother is. They must have been in on this together."

"She had me completely fooled. I really thought she cared for Robbie. She's good," the sheriff muttered. "The night of the party, Adam must have been the one driving the red car that took Robbie away. That's why he had Robbie's hat in the picture."

They entered the cell area where Adam was lying on the bunk. He looked up, scowled, and closed his eyes. The sheriff walked up to the bars of the cell and banged on them. The prisoner opened his eyes and glared at the two men.

"You have two choices here," the sheriff started. "Your sister is now on the run. We know it was her who poisoned Phil and laced the food at the party. She will go down for murder. If you cooperate and tell us where Robbie is, we will tell the judge you helped save a man's life."

Silence.

"Do you know what they do to cops in jail?" Jay asked. "Tell us where my brother is, and I will recommend that you are kept out of the general population."

"I hope my sister gets away. Your brother can rot where he is for all I care," Adam Cook hissed.

Roland shimmered into the corner of the cell area. Adam sat up, staring at the ghost.

I know where your brother is...

"Where is he Roland?" Jay asked.

Amy is at your brother's cottage and is talking on the phone to someone. She is driving the little red car I saw at the party, and she said she was going to the storage unit to finish him off...

"There's only one storage unit facility in town. Let's go," the sheriff announced.

14

Jay jumped into the cruiser with the sheriff. They switched on the lights and siren and sped to the outskirts of town where the Anchor Point Storage Facility was located. They pulled up to the gate. The sheriff signaled the employee to open the gates. There was only one car, a red car, inside the fenced-in area, and it was parked at the very end unit.

"We got her. There's no other way out," the sheriff announced.

Amy ran out of the unit as the cruisers approached. Heading for the back fence, she attempted to climb the chain-link fence to get out of the secure area. Jay was faster and grabbed her by the foot just as she was about to go over the top. He pulled her to the ground as she kicked and screamed in her attempt to get away.

Deputy Nickerson was right behind Jay and told him to go to his brother, that he would take care of the prisoner. Jay took off for the storage unit. His brother was inside, still dressed in the same leprechaun suit that he had worn at the party. He was lying on a cot with a thin blanket over him.

"Dude, what took you so long?" Robbie asked his brother weakly but smiling.

At that instant, Jay knew his brother would be okay. He smiled and knelt next to him. Robbie couldn't remember the last time that he had eaten, and he was shivering. The ambulance arrived, and Jay stepped aside so they could tend to his brother.

"I have to call my mom," Jay said to the sheriff.

He stepped outside the unit to make his call.

"Mom, we found him. We have Robbie."

"Tell her the paramedics are going to take him to the hospital, and she should meet us there," the sheriff said, coming up behind Jay. "They said he's going to be okay."

"Mom stop crying… I know you are his mother. He was at the storage facility. Yes, we caught who did this to him, and it was Amy and her brother. I know, I had a hard time believing it, too. I'll tell you the rest at the hospital."

He hung up as they were wheeling Robbie to the ambulance.

"I'm going to ride with my brother," Jay announced.

"We'll meet you at the hospital after we lock up Amy," the sheriff informed him. "I want to take Robbie's statement, personally."

Martha joined them in the emergency room. She kept crying as she hugged her son.

"You're getting my hospital gown all wet," Robbie announced as he hugged her back. "And I love you, too, Mom. Can you bring me some of your chowder? I'm starving."

"That's my son," Martha beamed.

The doctor told the family that Robbie would be staying overnight for observation. They wanted to make sure there would be no adverse reactions from the drugs they used to keep him sedated. The nurse piled on the blankets and promised the patient that food would be delivered shortly. Jay and Martha stayed while Robbie ate.

Sheriff Boyd arrived a short time later. Being warm and full, Robbie was tired and wanted to sleep. The sheriff agreed to take his statement in the morning and left.

"You get some sleep. We will be back early in the morning," his mom told him, pulling up the blankets over his shoulders.

"Bring some chowder," he replied, closing his eyes.

"I'll see you in the morning, dude," Jay said, glad to have his brother back.

"I knew you would find me. I never gave up on you," Robbie mumbled as he dozed off to sleep. "I love you, Jay."

Word traveled quickly around Anchor Point that Robbie had been found. Jay's cell phone rang constantly, but he answered every call. After making sure his mom got home okay, Jay opened a beer and settled down in front of a newly lit fire. The dogs had been fed and were curled up on the couch next to him.

Roland shimmered in next to the fireplace.

You found him...

"Yes, we did, thanks to you," Jay said, sitting up. "If you hadn't listened to what Amy was saying and let us know, Robbie would be dead right now. You saved his life, my friend," Jay stated.

He will be okay?

"He will. He's a little skinnier now than he was, but I am sure my mom will fatten him up," Jay answered. "I just wish I could tell the world that you saved my brother."

No need. You are like my family, and I couldn't bear to see Martha so sad.

"You are family," Jay assured the ghost. "And Robbie's hero."

I'm sorry it was Amy. Robbie really loved her.

"She fooled us all. Robbie will find someone again, I'm sure," Jay replied.

Just like you have found Susan.

"Yes, Roland, just like I have found Susan, and I need to tell her that."

May I visit Robbie tomorrow at his cottage?

"I'm sure he would be mad if you didn't."

Storm coming, I must return to the lighthouse...

"Thank you, again. You are my hero, too." Jay said, raising his bottle of beer in Roland's direction.

After four more beers and deciding to close the café tomorrow, Jay and the dogs went to bed. It was the first night in over a week that he got a decent night of sleep. The wind and snow whipped around outside, but Jay didn't hear a thing.

Roland stood his post on the catwalk protecting the ships from the storm, proud that he had saved his friend. Maybe this would help lighten the guilt he still felt over the shipwreck of The Fallen Mist. Maybe.

Martha brought her son home the following day. He insisted on staying in his own cottage to recuperate. His mother argued with him but to no avail. Robbie emphasized that he wanted to clean out Amy's personal belongings as soon as possible. Jay assured his mother he would check on his brother at least twice a day.

Roland visited Robbie every day for the next week, along with half the town. Jay had insisted that Robbie stay out of work for at least a week. He didn't fight the decision as he was still weak from the lack of food, and the drugs forced on him.

Jay was sitting up at the bar, having lunch. Robbie came for a visit to see how things were going as he would be returning to work the following night. Paul assured him that everything was ready for his return.

Several minutes later, the sheriff came to get some lunch.

"Robbie, you're looking good," the sheriff observed, sitting down on a barstool next to Jay.

"I'm feeling much better, thanks," he answered. "Are you here for my mom's chowder?"

"The biggest bowl you got," he replied, laughing. "It's mighty cold out there."

"Have you wrapped everything up?" Robbie inquired.

"Just about. Mary admitted to stealing jewelry from the store for John Smith to fence. Both her and John knew what Amy had planned, but never said anything to Stella. We are charging them as accomplices to murder as well as grand theft. Mary, John, Adam and Amy were going to take the money from the sale of the store and split it amongst themselves and not give Stella any of it."

"Are you saying Stella didn't have a clue about anything?" Jay asked, amazed.

"Nothing. They were going to take her for everything she had," the sheriff replied in between bites of chowder.

"I just don't understand how Amy could have done what she did to me," Robbie said, opening his beer.

"Revenge. It can over-take a person's thinking and drive them to do things they normally would not ever think of doing. Amy and Adam were so intent on getting even with their uncle for their father's state of life that they never knew that it wasn't even Phil that they should have been mad at. Mary took the money that Phil gave her to mail to his brother. He kept his word and never knew that his brother didn't receive the money."

"So, Phil died for nothing," Paul said, "Sad."

"Kidnapping Robbie was not part of the original plan," the sheriff added.

"I happened to turn around at the bar and saw Amy putting something in Phil's food. We were arguing out near the elevator area, and I got hit from behind. That's the last thing I remember until I woke up in the storage unit. Amy would visit once a day to make sure I was still drugged up and leave me a little water and sometimes some food. I was chained to the back wall and could barely get to the bucket they left for me to use as a bathroom."

"That means that Greg Peterson had nothing to do with the events either. He really just wanted to buy the building?" Jay asked.

"That's right," the sheriff agreed.

"Basically, it all came down to greed," Jay surmised.

"Yes, it did, and thank goodness no one else died from the other drugs that Amy put into the buffet food. Robbie, my friend, she is a vicious person, and you are lucky to be alive," the sheriff announced. "Thank our lucky stars for Roland. Not many people can say they were saved by a ghost."

"I'll never get mad at Roland for taking my stuff and hiding it again," Robbie said, laughing.

"One more question. Will Stella collect on Phil's insurance policy?" Jay asked.

"I don't know yet. She had nothing to do with his death, but I guess it is up to the insurance company whether they pay out or not. She is going to sell the store to Peterson as she wants to move far away from here."

"You really can't blame her," Jay agreed.

"Take it easy, Robbie," the sheriff said, standing up to leave. "Glad you are still with us.'

"Me, too, sheriff, Me, too."

"Back to work. The bills are not going to pay themselves," Jay stated. "Robbie, I'll see you tomorrow night. Go home and rest up for work. It will be a long night your first night back."

"I'm going to steal a few beers to take with me."

"How many times do I have to tell you and Mom? Borrow with no intent to return. It sounds better," Jay snickered as he walked away.

Jay waved to Robbie as he left through the kitchen.

He has no clue what he's walking into tomorrow night.

15

The parking lot of the café was full by five o'clock. Robbie walked in the back door and punched in. Susan said hi, smiled her usual bright smile and giggled a little.

"What's so funny?" Robbie asked.

"Nothing. I'm just so happy to see you back to work," she answered. "ORDER UP!"

Robbie grabbed his inventory clipboard and headed for the stairs to the bar. As he reached the top, a loud "surprise" greeted his ears. He looked around the room, and all his friends were there to greet him. Even the homeless people that he had helped over the years were there wearing big smiles from ear to ear.

"What is going on?" he asked, still looking from face to face.

The sheriff walked forward and stood next to Robbie.

"Tonight, my friend, you will not be working. Tonight, we are celebrating the return of Robbie. We know that you do everything you do for the homeless community here on Anchor Point in secret. We know that you don't like to be acknowledged for what you do. You are one of the most respected people of this community even though you may not realize it."

"I just do it because I can," he replied.

"We want you to continue what you do. The Robbie Hallett Community Fund has been set up for you to continue your work. The people of this community have donated all week, and you have a hefty balance to resume your work with the people you help," the sheriff announced.

"I don't know what to say," Robbie stuttered.

"You don't have to say anything. Here's to Robbie," the sheriff said, holding up his beer. "We're glad you are back with us."

"Here! Here!" chorused around the room.

"Everyone, help yourself to the buffet, and I promise this time there is nothing in the food," Jay announced.

Martha hugged her son and congratulated him after telling him how proud she was of him. Susa had come from the kitchen and gave him a quick hug. People started to gather around him, so the family members backed off and let Robbie enjoy the spotlight that he so rightly deserved.

Martha wandered off to mingle and eat, leaving Jay and Susan standing together alone.

"I'm sorry about how things worked out with Adam," Jay started.

"I'm not. After the first date, I knew he wasn't the right man for me," Susan admitted.

"I'm not going to lie. I was jealous when I saw you with him," Jay admitted.

"Just being jealous doesn't cut it, Jay," Susan started to say.

He slid his arm around her waist and pulled her close.

"I'm sorry that it has taken me so long to admit my feelings for you. I do love you, and I guess I didn't realize just how much until I saw you with someone else," Jay explained.

"Does this mean we are together again? I can't take much more of this on again off again thing," Susan told him.

"What do you think?" he asked as he pulled her in and kissed her.

"I guess that answers my question. Let's get some food. I hear they have an awesome chef that cooks here," Susann said, smiling and taking Jay's hand.

Roland was hiding in the corner watching them. He smiled when he saw Susan take Jay's hand and shimmered out.

The couple filled their plates and circulated while they ate. Robbie joined them and was glad that they were back together again.

"I forgot to tell you. Roland showed me another tunnel under the point. It may lead to the treasure as it has the clues hidden in it that are in the journal. I couldn't keep going in the tunnel without you, though. What say we go treasure hunting this coming Monday?" Jay asked.

"Sounds good to me. You know I appreciate all this tonight, but a party? Really? That's how I disappeared in the first place. I was going to swear off parties for a while," Robbie stated. "And women, no offense Susan."

"I give that until tomorrow night when you are right back behind the bar flirting with every woman who smiles at you,' Jay laughed.

"I guess you're right," Robbie agreed. "Let's party!"

The End

RECIPES

COLONIAL MAPLE BUTTER

¼ pound unsalted butter, at room temperature
1 teaspoon grated lemon peel
3 tablespoons real maple syrup

Blend all ingredients until smooth. Refrigerate for at least one hour before serving.

ORANGE BLOSSOM BUTTER

1 fresh orange
½ pound unsalted butter at room temperature
4 tablespoons of Grand Marnier liquor

Cut the whole orange (peel and all) into quarters-remove seeds.

Process orange in a blender or food processor until finely grated into a rough puree.

Mix orange, butter, and liquor until smooth. Chill for an hour before serving.

CAPE COD CLAM CAKES

2 eggs
2 - 7 ½ ounce cans of minced clams (liquid strained out and discarded)
2 cups of flour 1 cup of milk
½ teaspoon salt
¼ teaspoon pepper
2 teaspoons baking powder

Combine all dry ingredients. Mix in eggs and milk to form a batter. Stir in clams, mixing thoroughly. Drop one tablespoon at a time into deep hot oil and cook for 1 minute or until golden brown on both sides.

Richer clam flavor can be achieved by substituting ½ cup clam liquid and reducing milk by ½ cup.

Recipe serves four.

MAPLE APPLE SWEET POTATOES

4 to 5 medium sweet potatoes boiled in their skins
4 to 5 medium apples (granny smith work best)
1 cup maple syrup
¼ cup butter
Pinch of salt

Boil sweet potatoes in salted water. Slice apples into syrup. Add the butter and a pinch of salt. Cook gently until apples are tender.

Peel the cooked sweet potatoes and slice, putting half of them in a well-buttered baking dish. Spoon half of the apple mixture over them. Repeat the two layers and top with buttered crumbs.

Bake at 400 degrees long enough to heat thoroughly and brown the crumbs.

CRUMB MIXTURE

1 cup of brown sugar
½ cup of oats
½ cup of melted butter

Mix until all ingredients are moist.

OTHER BOOKS BY DONNA WALO CLANCY

THE JELLY SHOP MYSTERIES
Jellies, Jams, and Bodies
Jam Up and Jelly Fright
Christmas Jamboree
Until Jam Do Us Part

Coming in 2020
Pumpkin Butter Poison
Sleigh Bells Ring, Jelly's Cooking

THE SHIPWRECK CAFÉ MYSTERIES
Death by Chowder
Seashells and Christmas Bells
Death on the Half Shell

THELMA AND JUNE'S MYSTERY ADVENTURES
Death by Dauber

Coming in 2020
Bingo on the High Seas

Coming in 2021
Bingo Bag Mix-up
Weekend Wine Time

STANDALONES

The Baby Factory

The Wishing Cradle

Keep the Faith, Ellen McGuire

Also Coming in 2020

The Whiskey Barrel Ghost (October 2020)

Be Careful What You Wish For, Ellen McGuire (#2 in the series)

Dad's Final Gift (Christmas 2020)

Made in the USA
Middletown, DE
26 July 2020